Second Chance Scottish

A HOLIDAY NOVELLA

TRICIA O'MALLEY

LOVEWRITE PUBLISHING

Scottish Glossary

Tetchy: crabby, cranky, moody

Bloody: a word used to add emphasis; expletive

Wheesht (haud your wheesht): be quiet, hush, shut up

Bonnie: pretty

Och: used to express many emotions, typically surprise, regret, or disbelief.

Peely-wally: pale and sickly in appearance

Wee: small, little

Bit 'o banter: Scots love to tease each other, banter is highly cherished

Nae bother: It's no problem

"Life and love go on ... let the music play."
Johnny Cash

One

SKYE

There are two kinds of people who show up at a small bed and breakfast in a tiny off-the-beaten-track village the week before Christmas.

The first? Cheerful, adoring couples in matching wool sweaters who want mulled wine, fairy lights, and someone else to make their porridge in the morning.

The second? Those *pretending* to be cheerful, whose Christmas sweaters are nowhere in sight, who cringe at rooms filled with fairy lights, and who wouldn't be awake before breakfast has been served to know there was porridge on the menu. In other words, those who were running away from something.

The man at my check-in desk was definitely the second kind.

The fact that he kept his head ducked and his hat was

pulled low over his face pinged my radar before I even walked behind the small desk to greet him.

I grimaced at the sight of a guitar case at his feet, memories of long ago washing over me, and I kept my head down as I paged through my reservations book.

"Reservation for John Smith," he said, voice low, leaning forward over the desk. Something in his voice sent a shiver down my back, but I brushed it away, putting my customer service smile on.

"John Smith," I murmured, flipping to his reservation page. I'd been excited to get a last-minute booking. The winter months were my slowest, and I'd been more than happy to accommodate a month-long reservation.

His eyes lifted, just enough for me to get a good look. And that's when the ground fell out from under me.

What. The. Hell.

Of course the universe would deliver my ex-boyfriend—the one who wrote a number-one single about breaking my heart—directly to my inn during the loneliest time of the year.

Noah Byrne.

Ex-boyfriend.

Arsehole.

Because clearly, the universe had a sense of humor and it was cruel.

I gripped the edge of the desk to stop my hands from shaking. "No."

He blinked, an eyebrow winging up slightly. "No?"

"No, as in, no, Noah, *you* can't stay here. I don't care if you book under John Smith, Santa Claus, or King of Bloody England. Pick your guitar up and get out."

He gave me a slow once-over, and it felt exactly like it had fifteen years ago when we were rehearsing in a freezing garage. He'd looked at me like I was both his favorite song and the mistake he was about to make. My skin prickled with awareness and irritation.

"Hello to you too, Skye," he said finally. His voice hadn't changed. Still that husky, broken-in leather kind of sound that could make women scream or sob, depending on the chorus.

I hated that my knees went soft. I hated it more that I noticed he looked better now—taller somehow, broader, jaw shadowed with stubble. A few grays threaded his hair at his temples and somehow that made him even sexier.

But his eyes looked world weary, and *oh so* tired.

And I hated most of all that part of me wanted to ask if he was okay.

"Out," I repeated, keeping my voice flat.

"Booked for a month," he countered. *Did he think we were haggling over the price of a pint?*

How had I missed his name on the credit card I'd taken for this booking? Sliding a look at the reservation, I saw a different name—Matt—whose name was on the credit card for the booking. At the time, I'd assumed it was likely John Smith's partner.

"Who's Matt?"

"My agent."

"You can't stay here," I said, frustrated.

"I thought the booking was non-refundable? Can you afford to turn away guests?"

His question stung, mostly because it was true that the inn couldn't afford to hemorrhage cancellations. I'd inherited this place after my gran had passed and keeping it alive had become equal parts pride and punishment.

Still, I wasn't about to roll out the red carpet for Noah Byrne.

"You tricked me," I said.

"You wouldn't have let me book otherwise."

"Aye, you've got the right of that," I snapped.

I glared at him across the counter. Christmas music played softly from my Spotify playlist, an inane song about a snowman looking for his nose, and outside, an icy blast of wind rattled the windows. The small village of Kingsbarns carried on as if the world hadn't just tilted off its axis. *Why him? Why now?* Why here? *He could go anywhere in the world.*

Despite the warning bells going off in my head, I looked closer. Fatigue radiated in tension lines crossing his forehead and shadows smudged his eyes. This was a different category of tired. Not rock-star-on-tour tired. Not hungover tired. *Soul* tired.

And damn it, that's what made me hesitate.

One look. That was all it took. His eyes, heavy with things I didn't want to name, broke through my armor in the same way his songs had all those years ago.

Except for one song.

The song that cracked my heart open and spilled my vulnerabilities for the world to see.

He'd even had the gall to name it after me.

Skye.

The song the entire bloody world had sung along to while I'd tried to buy milk at the co-op without crying.

I'd hated him for writing it … and hated myself for knowing he hadn't been wrong.

I dragged in a breath. "One week," I said.

His mouth quirked. "The reservation's for a month."

"Take it or leave it."

"I'll take it." He looked down briefly and toed the guitar case, shrugging in that nonchalant way he had.

Seemed like disaster had just checked in.

By the time I'd handed him his key, his silence matching my own, my nerves were stretched as tight as a guitar string ready to be plucked. A thousand thoughts crowded my head, but I hated that the one that rose to the top was the one I'd tried to bury the deepest.

I've missed you.

"You're in room three. First floor, end of the hallway," I said. "Tea's on from four to half six."

Noah grunted in response and then left without another word, having to carry his guitar in front of him to trudge up the narrow stairwell. I listened to his footsteps down the hallway, each step dropping like intro beats to a song, and tried to breathe normally.

Noah Byrne.

My first love. And my biggest heartbreak.

Which was saying something, given I'd been married and divorced since I'd last seen Noah.

Plopping my chin in my fist, I gazed out the wide front window that overlooked the wee village. Kingsbarns in December was small, cold, and nosy. It's the place where everyone knew when you changed your curtains, much less when your rock star ex-boyfriend slunk back into town.

By the time Noah carried his guitar upstairs, my

phone had already buzzed with three text messages. Esther, the leader of a slightly terrifying group of busybody readers who called themselves the Book Bitches, lived across the road and had a front-row view of the ongoings at the inn. The Book Bitches would demand details. There was no escaping those matchmaking terrorists. When they weren't discussing the week's smutty book club read, they fancied themselves champions of lonely hearts. And by tomorrow, the whole village would be whispering that Skye Kerrigan had taken Noah Byrne back into her bed.

Which, by the way, would absolutely *not* happen.

I'd started my life over several times since I'd walked away from Noah Byrne with a broken heart and the wobbling conviction of a twenty-two-year-old, uncertain if she'd thrown away the best thing that ever happened to her. I'd gone home and started to work at my gran's inn. I met a "nice" man that I thought I could have a "nice" quiet life with until the silence had grown too loud to bear. We'd divorced, and I'd started over once more. Gran, my North Star, passed and while in the depths of grief, my life trajectory changed again. *I was fully responsible for this inn's success now.*

Life was simply that, though. A series of new beginnings, new directions, and new priorities. Sometimes they hurt. Sometimes they were the best thing that happened to you. But with Noah being here now? At thirty-seven, I was older than the wide-eyed girl I'd been when we'd first dated. I was too tired, and too busy keeping the inn from falling apart to play his redemption arc.

I snorted at my thoughts.

That was quite a leap for me to assume he was coming back to town to reconnect with me.

Why was he really here?

The inn smelled faintly of cinnamon and pine from the wreaths I'd hung earlier, but the electrics needed updating, the kitchen pipes rattled every time I turned on the hot tap, and the accounts I'd stayed up late with last night still made my stomach hurt. Which meant, I had no time for daydreaming about memories best kept to the past. I had a room to turn over, guest inquiries to answer, and laundry to change out. Pushing thoughts of Noah Byrne aside, I bent my head to my tasks.

Four o'clock brought tea in the lounge and I held my breath as I carried in a tray of shortbread and mince pies, setting it down on a low table beneath the window. Pretending not to notice the shadow leaning against the mantel, I looked around the room I'd once been so proud of and tried to see it through a rich person's eyes.

Faded floral wallpaper peeled at the corners, and two rose-colored loveseats were pulled close to the fireplace, where a cheerful fire crackled. Four bistro tables with two chairs each were tucked on the other side of the room under the windows that overlooked the main street, and each table had a decorative teacup with a few buds of fresh flowers as a centerpiece. Music played quietly in the background, the requisite Christmas melodies, and several squat candles flickered over the mantel.

It was worn, but well-loved, and I lifted my chin higher.

Noah was watching the fire, sleeves pushed up, hair falling into his eyes. He looked almost normal—like any other man who'd wandered in from the cold. Except normal men didn't leave heartbreak songs in their wake *... and didn't still make my chest ache with longing.*

"You should cut your hair," I said, because silence was worse.

"You used to like it long."

"I used to like a lot of things about you."

He glanced at me then, quick and sharp. For a moment, something like regret flickered, but before he could reply, the front door banged open.

"Skye, love!" Esther's voice echoed through the hall. "You'll never believe who I thought I saw today—"

As she entered the lounge, eyes landing square on Noah, she froze. Smiled. And then grinned like the cat who'd got into the cream.

"Och," she said, looking between me and Noah. "Oh, this is going to be fun."

And just like that, I knew the Book Bitches had a brand-new project.

Two

NOAH

Scandals don't always strike violently like lightning. Sometimes they creep in.

They rot you from the inside out like damp in an old wall.

By the time the gossip blogs caught wind, the whole structure was already compromised.

I should've known. Hell, maybe I *did* know. The late-night calls Glen took in the next room, hushed voices and the way he carefully angled his laptop out of my sight. The assistants who stopped meeting my eye when I asked about the books. The accounts that didn't balance no matter how many times I ran the numbers myself.

I'd told myself it was fine. That Glen was looking out for us, like always. That he'd been the one who pulled us from pubs into arenas, from sticky-floored clubs into stadiums. That I owed him my loyalty.

And now? Words like *embezzlement*, *tax fraud*, *gambling debt* shrouded my emails from the attorneys. The tabloids wouldn't be far behind ... like sharks scenting blood. None of this was attached to my name—*yet*—but it was close enough that I could feel their teeth.

So I ran.

Not to LA. Not to London. Not to the glass-walled apartments or rented villas where people like me usually disappeared to.

I ran here.

To Kingsbarns. To the one place I hadn't set foot in for years. The only place that I had ever really felt like *me*.

And straight into Skye Kerrigan's line of fire.

"Now, what's all this then?"

Esther was a tiny woman with shock-white hair, a questionable taste in jumpers, and eyes that missed nothing. The years fell away, and I warmed inside, remembering how she used to scold me for one thing or another and then feed me extra biscuits. Esther and her cronies were a central part of my childhood, having kept a watchful eye over me and the group of kids that roamed the streets looking for trouble in a town that delivered none.

"Would you look at that?" Esther asked, voice high with delight. "Noah Byrne, skulking back into Kingsbarns after all these years. Into Skye's inn, no less? Och, I'll be damned."

"Esther," Skye warned, tone clipped.

Her voice still sent a shiver across the back of my neck. It always had. Her long ginger hair—a few silver threads now mingling with her curls—was clipped back with a bright pink hair clip. A colorful beaded necklace twined with a gold chain at her neck, and a few lines edged her bonnie blue eyes.

She'd never looked prettier.

Esther ignored her. "What are you doing back? Come to make amends? Or stir up trouble? Because I'll tell you plain, boyo, if you break her heart again, you'll answer to me. And the book club."

Skye's cheeks pinkened and she pressed a hand to her mouth.

Had I broken her heart? Or had she broken mine? The truth probably fell somewhere in the middle, but this was neither the time nor the place to peel those layers back.

I pinched the bridge of my nose. "Good to see you too, Esther. Can I say, you look as fresh as a meadow after a morning spring rain?" I gave her one of my renowned Noah Byrne grins and raised an eyebrow for good measure.

Esther's eyes narrowed and then she cackled. "Och, cheeky as ever. But thinner. Too thin. And not in a healthy way." She squinted. "Rumor says your manager's in deep muck. Gambling, fraud, the works. That true, then?"

Skye started, rounding on me, her eyes wide. I winced.

Heat crawled up my neck. So the gossip blogs had started already. "Don't believe everything you read."

"Meaning it's true."

"Meaning it's none of your business."

Skye glanced to the front hallway, looking nervous. "That's enough, Esther. The other guests will be coming down soon."

Esther planted herself like a wartime bunker. "Don't

hush me, lass. Someone's got to keep this boy honest. You think the whole village won't know by morning? My phone's already buzzing."

"Esther." Skye's voice had a brittle edge. "Out."

Esther sniffed, satisfied she'd planted her flag. "Fine, fine. But mark me, Noah Byrne, mess with our girl here, and you'll have hell to pay. This is no encore tour. This is real life."

And with that, she swept out, muttering something about emergency book club meetings and extra wine.

Silence collapsed over the room.

I sank onto the sofa, staring at the flames. "Friendly as ever."

"You deserved worse," Skye said, shutting the door firmly.

She wasn't wrong.

Skye had always seen what I couldn't.

"Glen's a shark, Noah," she said, pacing our tiny kitchen, hair wild around her face. "Och, he doesn't care about the music. He doesn't care about our music. He wants control. He'll bleed us dry."

"He believes in us."

"Bollocks. Glen believes in himself. And when he's finished, he'll throw you away."

I laughed. Hard. "We'll prove you wrong."

Her silence was worse than shouting. She looked at me— the desolate look in her eyes searing my heart—and said, "Then you've already chosen him over me. Over us."

And she'd walked.

We were twenty-two, exhausted, raw from too many gigs and too little money.

We'd just been offered our first real contract. Not just a small-time record deal, not just a pub tour. The real thing. Big stages. Big money. A manager who had promised the world.

I'd thought it was everything. She'd thought the contract seemed dodgy and had hated how our manager had dismissed her questions.

It was the night we broke.

And I'd replayed her words over and over throughout the years.

I'd told myself I'd write her a song, and that it would fix everything. That she'd hear it and come back and realize what she was missing out on. But *Skye* wasn't an apology song. It was a wound I poured salt into and sold for ninety-nine pence a download.

It hit number one. Stadiums sang her name back at me, my own personal torture.

And she hated me for it. *And judging from her current expression, that was still the case.*

"I've changed my mind. You can't stay here," she said, arms crossed, chin tilted in that way that had once unraveled me.

"Too late, I'm already unpacked."

"You didn't even bring a bag," Skye protested.

I had, but she hadn't been around when I'd slipped back down and retrieved it from where I'd left it outside, unsure if she'd actually let me in.

"You told me one week."

"I don't think it's a good idea." Skye shook her head.

"You can give me a week."

"I don't have to give you anything, Noah Byrne." Skye glowered, clearly unhappy.

"No, lass, you don't. But I'd be mighty grateful if you did." I tried my best puppy dog eyes and was rewarded when she rolled her eyes in return.

"I shouldn't be doing this," Skye said to herself, and hope bloomed. Stomping out of the room, she came back with a pen and paper, scribbling furiously. "House rules," she said, shoving it at me.

"No music after ten. No smoking. No overnight guests. No songs about Skye. No touching." At that, I raised an eyebrow at Skye and her face flushed.

"And no paparazzi," Skye added.

My mouth twitched. "How exactly am I supposed to enforce that?"

"You figure it out."

"Bit harsh."

Her eyes glittered. "If you don't like it, there are other inns."

There weren't. Not in Kingsbarns at Christmas, with St. Andrews overrun and every B&B booked out by families and tourists. She knew it. I knew it.

I leaned back, studying her. Older, sharper, steadier. Not the girl I'd left behind, but the woman she'd become.

"You've changed," I said.

Her laugh was short, sharp, and sliced through me. "And you haven't. That's the problem."

"I have, but you just don't see it yet." At least I hoped that was true. I was worlds apart from the boy who hadn't been strong enough to stand up for Skye and fight for a better contract for the both of us. What would our lives have been like if she'd been out there? Singing by my side the world over?

Skye shifted, her eyes going to the fire. "Is it true? Did he screw you over?"

"Seems that way." It felt like swallowing razor blades to admit it, but it was only fair that I gave Skye her due. She'd been right about the dodgy manager all along.

"I'm sorry for that." Skye stood, glancing toward the front room as voices sounded on the stairs. "It doesn't exactly make me happy to have been right about him."

This wasn't the time for a deeper conversation, and I wasn't sure either of us was ready to have one. Instead, I pulled my hat low over my head and snagged some short-bread to take back to my room, breezing past the guests who had gathered in the foyer.

Later, upstairs in the small room with its slanted ceiling and creaking radiator, I stared at the paper in my hands.

House rules.

Clearly created solely for me. *Really, Skye?* It was as if she felt she could articulate fifteen years of anger into bullet points. Like she could build a fence high enough to keep me out. *I know you hate me, lass.*

I'd told myself I was only here because of the circulating scandal ... because I needed a safe, quiet place to hide.

Lies. Utter rubbish, Byrne.

But the truth was, I'd missed Skye terribly. Though time separated us, softening the sting of our pain, I'd never stopped thinking about her. There were so many times I'd almost picked up the phone to call her but then remembered she didn't want me to. She'd moved on. Started her life over. And I'd had no place in it at all. That part had burned the worst, I supposed. I'd gone from being the most important person in Skye's life to her most loathed.

Still, I'd come back here, to Kingsbarns, the moment I needed refuge.

Old habits do die hard, I guess.

Because even if she hated me, even if she never forgave me, Kingsbarns was the only place that had ever been my home. And Skye Kerrigan—the girl with a voice like wildfire—was the only person who had ever seen me for who I really was.

And, bloody hell, I still wanted her.

Three

SKYE

Running a bed and breakfast in December was like being slowly choked by tinsel.

On good days, it was cozy, charming, the kind of place tourists wrote glowing reviews about on TripAdvisor. On bad days, like today, it felt like living in a snow globe someone wouldn't stop shaking. Guests ringing bells, candles burning too sweet, laundry multiplying like rabbits. And, worst of all, Noah bloody Byrne upstairs, turning every breath I took into an act of self-control.

By nine that night, I'd had enough.

Enough of cinnamon and pine-scented candles, enough of folding pillowcases, enough of pretending the sound of floorboards creaking above me wasn't the man I'd once loved pacing around in boots.

I told myself I needed to do a nightly inspection of the

village seasonal decor, a game where I gave scores to the neighborhood Christmas decorations, but what I really needed was out. Out of this bed and breakfast, perhaps out of Kingsbarns, but definitely out and away from my past that had come back to haunt me. I pulled on my coat, jammed a beanie over hair that had given up hours ago, and escaped into the bitter cold that makes your teeth hurt.

Kingsbarns at night is all stone and salt. The sea sits just beyond the dark, a permanent, patient friend. Or foe, depending on its mood. A window glowed with a tree strung in warm white lights—tasteful—and two doors down the Jamiesons had a reindeer that blinked like a migraine—less tasteful. I loved them both. The air smelled of smoke from the fires and salt from the ocean. It should have calmed me. *This* was familiar. My place, my town, my people.

Not Noah's.

He'd given up on me, on all of us, long ago.

Not that it stopped people from bragging that *the* Noah Byrne had once lived here. I was surprised they hadn't put a plaque up at his old house. This village dearly loved a good commemorative sign.

My feet picked the way for me, following the same path instinctively. A left past the phone box that never works, another left where the pavement buckles, and then the sign swung into view, laughter and voices drifting from the door that was just closing behind a patron.

The Royal Unicorn.

The local pub, which grounded Kingsbarns, was the meeting point for all major discussions, and had recently undergone a renovation when Harper, an American, had come to Kingsbarns thinking she was going to get a pub experience for a couple of weeks. Instead, she'd ended up with a boyfriend, a wee warrior kitten named Wallace, and a pub renovation on her hands. In the end, Kingsbarns had a refurbished pub, I had a new friend in Harper, and we'd all been happier for it.

I paused with a hand on the door, took one last lungful of cold wintry air, and went inside.

Warmth slid over me. The beams that crossed the ceiling were older than everybody in the room combined and were currently draped in tinsel the color of Christmas memories. Fairy lights looped along the bar mirror, turning the bottles that lined the shelves into their own pretty holiday display. The pub was doing a fairly bustling business tonight, with most tables filled, and I raised a hand as people greeted me.

Wallace was curled at the edge of the bar, his tail lazily batting a picture frame of Lewis, the former owner of the pub who had passed and left the business to his grandson, Reed. A dram of whisky sat in front of the stool left empty for Lewis, and a pang of nostalgia for Gran hit my heart.

I almost turned right back around, unsure if I was really in the mood to socialize, but going back meant the inn. The inn meant Noah.

"Skye!"

Of course.

Esther's voice hit me like a snowball. She was at a table in the corner with the Book Bitches, who were as sparkly as the Christmas decorations that lined the windows of the pub. Three of them wore sequined hats, Shannon had antlers on, and Cherise wore a jumper with a T-Rex decorated in ornaments.

Tree-rex, I read and smiled. Despite my mood I went over to them and looked at the damage they'd done on their table. An empty wine bottle was next to another wine bottle that was already half drunk, and five empty shot glasses were lined up like misbehaving children.

I pasted on a smile and slid into a chair because saying "no" to the Book Bitches is like saying "no" to gravity.

"Evening," I said.

"Evening, she says," Meredith murmured, eyes a touch too bright. "Look at her. That's a woman who needs a glass the size of her face."

Shannon shoved a glass toward me. "It's a Malbec. It was a Merlot before that, and a respectable pinot before that, but the pinot couldn't keep up."

"What's with the hats?" I asked, nodding at the sequined caps.

"You like? We're trying something new." Shannon tugged the brim and pulled it at a cheeky angle over her face.

Cherise pushed the mince pies across. "Eat. You're peely-wally."

"I am not peely-wally," I lied, but I reached for a mince pie anyway. "I am ... seasonally translucent."

Esther's eyes narrowed and then she smiled sweetly. "Rough day?"

"You know how radiators develop personalities? One became a soprano. Also, a guest used the microwave to dry socks."

"Monsters," Shannon said gravely. Her eyes cut sideways. "We heard a whisper."

"Of course you did." I sipped and glared at Esther who looked up at the ceiling. "What whisper, precisely?"

"That a certain man checked into your inn under the name *John Smith*," Meredith singsonged. "For all the songs he writes, you would think he would be more imaginative."

"You'd think. But who cares, right? It's not that big a deal," I said, as if I hadn't spent all evening pretending I couldn't hear the weight of his footsteps upstairs.

"Mm." Esther's hum said she'd allow my delusion as a treat. "Well, if you want us to fight off the paparazzi when they arrive, we can."

"I've been doing cardio kickboxing classes," Cherise added. She flexed a somewhat wobbly arm. "From a YouTube class."

"I'm good with kitchen shears," Esther promised me.

"Good to know. Also, please don't maim people," I said, trying to change the subject from the one man I was desperately trying not to think about. "How's the Christmas charity raffle going?"

"Better since we added Gregory's calendar," Shannon said cheerfully.

"You made Gregory do a calendar?" I choked. Gregory worked in the local government office and was an unofficial Book Bitch. He tended to wear beige sweaters and loved crossword puzzles.

"He insisted," Meredith said. "He's 'Mr. January' and 'Mr. June,' due to scheduling issues and the fact we liked those photos best."

"Is he ... covered?" I asked. *Please, God, let him be covered.*

"Strategic baubles," Esther said, winking at me. "Don't be a prude."

I laughed in spite of myself. The Book Bitches had a way of plucking me out of my head and plonking me into a better mood, whether I liked it or not. The wine also helped. A little.

I was peeling the foil off a second mince pie, my back to the pub, when the door opened.

The pub didn't fall silent—that only happens in films —but the sound changed. It was thicker. Sharper. Like the air right before a lightning strike.

I glanced over my shoulder, already knowing.

Noah Byrne walked in.

He didn't belong in a place like this anymore, and somehow he fit anyway. Tall and confident yet pausing as though he needed permission to enter. The jacket was too thin for a Fife winter's night, the scruff that coated his jaw was a couple days past respectable, and his eyes glinted in the lights. He scanned the room and, of course, found me in seconds.

My insides did a thing I refused to name.

"Oh," Meredith breathed, not even pretending to be subtle. She fanned her face. "It's him."

"Behave," I hissed.

"Skye." Cherise's hand covered mine, warm and soft. "Breathe in. Breathe out."

"Would you stop? It's not a big deal. He's not a big deal." I broke eye contact, not interested in sparking any rumors that I was seen lusting after Noah Byrne in the local pub.

"I mean, he kind of is," she said.

"Not helping, Cherise," Esther said, scolding her. "Now, tell me, Skye. When was the last time you spoke to Noah?"

"A few hours ago when I served him tea," I reminded Esther and her gaze sharpened.

"You know what I meant. Before that?"

"Who can say, really?" I shrugged. Even though I remembered our last conversation like it was yesterday.

Esther leaned forward, her eyes narrowing. "So I'm going to take that as you're deliberately avoiding my questions, which means ..."

"You still care about him." Shannon leaned forward, her voice barely a stage whisper.

My cheeks flamed.

"Ladies, we've got our work cut out for us." Esther actually rubbed her hands together and I groaned, burying my face in my wine glass.

At the bar, Noah ordered a whisky, slid the glass between his fingers, and leaned back into his stool like he'd never left Kingsbarns. People were pretending not to stare.

Everyone was staring.

Harper shot me a questioning look from behind the bar. She didn't know our history, and likely didn't know much about Noah Byrne at all, but she could tell something was up.

The conversations picked up again, the noise swelling around me, cocooning me from Noah's presence mere feet away from where I clutched my wine glass so hard I was surprised it didn't shatter in my grip. I'd thought I'd moved on from Noah years ago, that I wouldn't be so affected by him, but it seemed I'd been lying to myself all this time. Our connection was electric, well at least it was on my end, and I swear my skin buzzed every time his gaze turned my way.

The radio switched songs, and I closed my eyes. Ice flooded my veins as the first unmistakable strum of *that* guitar riff growled through the speakers.

The opening chords of the song that had buzzed my life like a mosquito I just couldn't kill.

Skye.

The room shifted and every eye fell on me. Heads turned, mouths curved, a couple of women at the bar clapped their hands over their hearts as if they'd been waiting all night to hear it. I could feel heat rising up my throat, my eyes pricking.

Across the room, Noah didn't move. He watched me, his slate-gray eyes the color of a wintry ocean at dawn, the whisky glass clutched in his hand as his younger voice bled into the pub.

Skye, you were the wildfire I couldn't hold …

I could've handled a breakup song, if he'd kept it vague. But he'd named me. He hadn't even bothered to give me a metaphor or a fake name like "Rose" or "June." He'd carved my actual name into radio history, and for over a decade I'd changed the station when the song had come on and pretended it hadn't gutted me.

At the table, the Book Bitches drew a collective breath.

"Bloody hell," Shannon said, hurriedly topping up my drink.

"What odd timing," Meredith murmured.

"I've always liked this song," Esther admitted, her tone apologetic. She surprised me by reaching over to squeeze my hand.

It felt like the room slowly dissolved around the edges.

Time blurred.

The pub, now. The garage, then.

Our last fight.

Me walking out because he wouldn't believe what I could already see happening.

Six months later I'd been sitting in traffic, on a trip back to, ironically, the Isle of Skye, where I'd gone to camp out, nurse my wounds, and get my head on straight, when the song had come on the radio.

Those intro chords had me pulling my car to the side of the road, my hands gripping the wheel so tightly the skin at my knuckles had gone white.

My name, thrown back at me, crooning through my car speakers.

And I, idiot that I was, had felt both fury and gratitude that he'd ever loved me enough to write it. The latter emotion I'd never shared with anyone.

The song had exploded.

It was everywhere.

Impossible to avoid, I'd had to lock down my emotions as Noah's stardom had risen off the back of the song that bore my name.

The co-op queue, months later, two teenagers humming it behind me, one saying, "Imagine being her."

A graduation party I bartended for cash when the inn's books looked grim and the song had come on. A group of women swaying, crying, no idea that the woman refilling their Prosecco flinched every time the chorus hit.

And now here, the village I'd chosen over touring vans and dirty green rooms, pinning me to the wall with my own name.

My body moved before my brain. I stood so fast I banged my knee, the glasses clinked, and wine sloshed.

"Skye—" Esther started.

But I was already out of the booth, threading through bodies, avoiding his look, ignoring my name. The chorus began, and I hit the door at a run.

Outside, winter grabbed my face and held it, and I gulped air so sharp it burned the back of my throat. The surf was a low growl beyond the dark. A light over the community center door flickered like a warning.

You're fine. It's fine. This is fine.

Behind me, the song rolled on, as relentless as the tide, growing louder as the door opened and slammed shut.

"Skye."

He didn't get to say my name like that. Low and rough and full of history.

I turned anyway.

Noah stood under the pub's sign, lamplight cutting his face into planes. He hadn't bothered buttoning his coat. The whisky was still in his hand, the glass catching fairy lights like a tiny, breakable planet.

"You shouldn't have followed me," I said.

"You shouldn't have run then."

"Run?" I laughed, and it wasn't a nice sound. "Your bloody anthem starts blaring and you think I should stay there and subject myself to it?"

He flinched, minutely, like I'd flicked a finger at a bruise. "I'd have switched it off if I could."

"You can't switch off things you put into the world," I said. "That's the problem, isn't it? You press 'release' and then the rest of us just have to live with it."

He took that, let it hit, but didn't parry. His breath fogged in front of him. Somewhere behind us, someone whooped, and the chorus faded into the next verse like a bad idea you kept indulging. Kind of like this conversation with Noah.

"I wrote it because I loved you," he said, finally.

The worst part about Noah Byrne is that sometimes he meant what he said.

"I know." The wind flicked hair into my mouth, and I shoved it away. "That's why it hurt."

A beat. Two. We stood there like stupid statues while the village went on being itself around us—a car door slamming, a dog pulling its person down the lane, the wind shaking the trees.

"You look tired," I said, because apparently I prefer small talk to open arteries.

He huffed. "I'm fine."

"Liar."

His mouth curved, exhausted. "You always did call me on my crap."

"Perk of being the one who knew you before you were ... whatever it is you are now."

He looked past me to where the dark fields began, his voice flattening. "I'm still me."

"Mm." I crossed my arms to keep from reaching for

him. "Tell that to the version of you that signed with a man I told you not to trust."

"That's not fair."

"Neither is life."

"Skye—"

"No." I lifted a hand. "We're not rehashing old history on the footpath outside The Royal Unicorn while someone murders *Fairytale of New York* inside."

The radio had moved off *Skye* and lurched into a Pogues cover that sounded like two cats fighting in a bag. I took it as divine commentary.

Or maybe it was the ghost that was rumored to still haunt the pub from time to time.

Noah scraped a hand over his jaw. His knuckles were red from the cold. "I came here because I needed ... because it was the only place that made sense."

"And by 'place' you mean—"

"You." His eyes were steady. Stupid man. Stupid, brave, honest man. "I meant you."

That guitar string of emotion plucked painfully, and it vibrated through me, the reverberations of what once was echoing through me.

"Good night, Noah." I swallowed against a lump that had formed in my throat, unable to speak anymore lest I start crying and knowing how I'd explain all of the emotions that whirled inside me.

"Skye—"

"Good. Night."

I turned and thankfully, he didn't follow. Unsurprising, given his past of not following me when I left, but maybe a tiny part of me had hoped he would. I sighed. It wasn't easy being so at odds with old hurts and what I wanted for myself now.

I didn't go home right away. I couldn't. The sea called to me, as it always had, inviting me to share my secrets, something I'd also always found comforting.

Cutting down the path by the church, I walked toward the dark ribbon where the fields fall away to sand. At the water's edge, I let the roar fill my head until there was room for exactly one thought.

I am not going to do this again.

I was not going to be twenty again and full of hope. Once upon a time, I'd believed in a fairy tale that said Noah and Skye would live happily ever after. We'd make beautiful music, we'd be a team, a family, and if fame found us, great, but if it didn't, we'd still be happy. But then everything changed and ...

And I grew up.

Even if there was a chance that Noah was here for me, I was not going to be a name in a song he threw to a crowd when he needed a climax. I was not going to make my life an afterthought to his.

I gave myself a mental pat on the back. There. Priorities sorted.

My phone buzzed in my coat pocket. Digging it out with fingers that had gone stiff from the cold, I checked the message from Esther.

Kitchen shears?

Despite my mood, I laughed.

Stand down, soldier. I'll be fine.

Copy that. Back to work on the charity fundraiser then. I've got your scarf by the way.

I'll get it tomorrow. Thanks.

I shoved the phone away and stared at where the moon-light rippled across the surface of the sea until the song in my head drained out and the wind stitched me back together enough to function.

By the time I trudged back into the village, the pub noise had hit a warm lull. Through the window I could see Gregory conducting a carol with exaggerated solemnity and the Book Bitches swaying dramatically. Noah was nowhere in the slice of view my nosiness allowed. For a second, I wondered if he'd left Kingsbarns already, if he'd walked into the night and kept going until London or oblivion.

Then the door opened, and he stepped out with his collar flipped up, and I remembered he was not courteous enough to evaporate.

He fell into step beside me, and neither of us spoke on the short walk back to the inn. My brief peace from the sea was shattered by every step he took next to me.

Back at the inn, I did what I always do when I don't know what to do … I cleaned things that weren't dirty. As soon as we stepped inside, I grabbed a broom from the closet and stepped into the lounge to sweep the already clean floors. Ignoring Noah's pause in the entryway, I stayed focused on my task, refusing to look up. Finally, after I re-cleaned the entire lounge and front entryway, I went into the kitchen and made tea, even though I wanted whisky, and sat at the kitchen table pretending chamomile could solve anything.

A floorboard creaked, and I looked up. Noah leaned in the open kitchen doorway, not crossing the threshold like we were in a vampire film. Sensible of him.

"I didn't want to leave it like that," he said. His voice. It was one of the first things that had attracted me to him. Smooth like whisky, but raspy as if he was growling. *Do not reminisce about who you were once.*

"Tough. That's how it's left."

"I'm sorry," he said, and I believed him, and that was almost worse. "For the song. For ... putting us out into the world like that. I can't fix that."

"Would you? If you could?" I stood, taking my cup to the counter, my insides buzzing with nerves.

"I ... I don't know." Noah sounded surprised. His words stung, but at least I could appreciate the truth of them. "*Skye* was such an integral part of launching my career. But it's always been this pivotal moment for me. Before *Skye* and after *Skye*."

My eyes pricked. He was talking about more than just the song.

If on the other side of the truth was that a part of me had applauded him for writing it. One of the reasons *Skye* had been so successful was because it had been blindingly honest. It takes courage for an artist to be that honest with his songs.

"I understand." A bit, at least. I didn't know what it was like to sing to stadiums full of people, but I did know how it felt to have before and after moments that defined my life. Before Noah and after Noah. Before divorce and after divorce.

"Let's just get through this week," I said, rinsing my cup, my back to him, forcing myself to gather my composure. What else was there to say? He'd apologized for the song that had shattered me all those years ago, and now what? There was nowhere to go from here.

"You make it sound like it's a penance," he said, and for once I had no smart remark.

Turning, I looked at him, needing him to go lest I do something stupid like cross the room and pull his mouth down to mine. Even after all these years, I couldn't deny the man still had unmistakable charisma. It followed him around the room, changing the molecules in the air as he moved, and hit me straight in my core.

"Good night, Noah."

He nodded once, like a man agreeing with a judge, then stepped back into the corridor. "Good night, Skye."

He left. The floorboard above creaked again minutes later, moving from one end of the room to the other.

I poured the rest of the water from the kettle out, flicked the lights off and stood there for a moment, because sometimes the dark is honest with you in a way the light refuses to be. Like when I'd lie awake at three in the morning and wonder if Noah ever missed me.

Shaking my head, I climbed the stairs and paused because, apparently, I liked to punish myself, and listened.

At first, nothing, then the brush of strings. Not a song. Just fingers testing a chord.

Yearning swelled, and I hurried up the stairs to my flat on the top floor and rushed through a basic bedtime routine. It wouldn't do me any good to think about *what ifs*. What if I had stayed with the band? With Noah? Would I, too, be a household name? Would playing my music on the world's stage have brought me joy?

In bed, the duvet smelled of laundry soap and loneliness, so I made a list in my head to put myself to sleep—buy a new washer hose, find a new plumber who wouldn't call me "hen" in a way that made me murderous, make extra scones for the Austrian tourists who were eating like locusts, delete *Skye* from Harper's playlist at the pub.

Tonight I'd been the woman who ran from a pub to escape the pain from a song written in her past. Tomorrow I'd be the woman who runs an inn like a boss and knows better, because at the end of the day, keeping the inn running was the only thing that I could control.

When I finally drifted, I dreamed of a garage, frosted breath, fingers raw from strings, with a boy looking at me like I was his future. I woke up with my jaw clenched and tears drying on my face.

Four

NOAH

Insomnia, thy name is Kingsbarns.

I spent the night lying on a mattress that felt like it had opinions about me, listening to the old house breathe. Radiators hissed and a floorboard squeaked every time someone crossed the hall.

By morning I'd achieved that special level of tired where your shadow looks hungover. Showering in hot water that alternated between "glacier melt" and "hell mouth," I made a mental note to sneak a look at Skye's boiler. My old man had been a plumber, and though it had been years since I'd done any work like that, I could still remember the basics.

I still hadn't turned my phone on, but one glance at my email on my laptop was enough for me to slam it with a resounding thud.

Bloody Glen.

He'd swept me away when I was too green to know any better, and though he'd delivered on his promises to make our band famous, he'd also, apparently, done a lot of shady things along the way. I'd given Glen too much signing power, believing that he'd always look out for our best interests, and it turns out, he'd had other motivations all along.

News of which, I was just finding out about.

Along with the rest of the world.

Too tetchy to face Skye this morning, I slipped past the lounge full of lodgers eating breakfast, a hat pulled low over my face, and stepped into the wintry morning sunshine. The faded light fell upon a place that held some of my happiest memories, and I headed for the bookshop that had once been my sanctuary when I wasn't fiddling around on my guitar, teasing out notes and avoiding chores.

Tucked down a small, sheltered lane, Highland Hearts Bookshop had a bell over the door and Christmas garlands strung along the edge of the roof. It looked like it had been freshened up recently, with a bright coat of paint on the door, and an intricate window display of woodland fae building a Christmas tree from a stack of books.

"That's inventive," I said, admiring the work, and pushed inside. The smell of books, a hint of cinnamon, and smoke from a woodburning stove greeted me and I sighed, feeling some of the tension that banded my shoulders ease. Bookshops had always been a refuge for me and Highland Hearts had been one of my first loves where I'd disappear to read about knights and elves and warriors on a quest.

A plush stag wearing a Santa hat stood on the counter next to signs that offered *Storytime with Rosie: Elves Who*

Make Bad Choices and *Harper's Holiday Romance Recs: Heroines that move abroad and fall in love.* Two women turned as I entered, Harper from the pub, and another I hadn't met yet. Harper had a fresh-faced beauty that only came from being wildly in love, and she smiled cheerfully at me.

"Oh, hello," Harper said, nudging the woman next to her whose smile made you want to hand over your secrets and your wallet. She wore a jumper that read BOOKS > BOYS, which I decided not to take personally. "Come meet, Rosie, the new owner of Highland Hearts."

"Good morning," Rosie said, with a tone that implied she'd had a lot of coffee. "If it isn't John Smith?"

I winced.

Harper snorted. "Sorry, Noah. Your secret's out."

Their eyes sized me up in a way that only women protective of their friends could do and I found myself hunching my shoulders.

Before I could reply, the bell chimed behind me.

Esther barreled inside, eyes glittering with either mischief or caffeine, wearing a jumper with what looked to be one reindeer mounting another. Behind her were the rest of the women, most I'd known since childhood, all in various lewd jumpers. The Book Bitches, assembled, the unofficial government of Kingsbarns.

They didn't look at me. Not at first. They were hunting bigger game.

"Where is Skye?" Esther demanded. I straightened. Skye was here? Shouldn't she be manning breakfast at the inn?

"Back room," Rosie said. "We've got her on wrapping

gifts for the charity Christmas tree. She's been arguing with the wrapping paper for ten minutes now."

"Good. We'll corner her there. Harper, you're with me. Shannon, get the biscuits. Meredith, give Gregory's calendar to Rosie to place by the till—no, not *that* photo, we don't want to get shut down. Cherise, fetch the donation tin."

"What's happening?" I asked.

"Intervention," Harper said, grabbing a roll of tape like a weapon. "Cozy, small-town, book-clubby, heavy-on-the-meddle intervention."

"For Skye?"

"For you," Rosie corrected sweetly. "By way of Skye."

Esther turned at the back doorway. "No running, Noah Byrne. We run faster."

There are a few sentences you don't hear backstage. That was one of them.

I followed because, apparently, I had misplaced bravery or debilitating fatigue. *Or both.*

The back room was controlled chaos. Strings of different colored twine had been placed next to bins of baubles and a stack of boxes waiting to be wrapped. Skye stood at a long table, hair twisted up, hands braced, looking at Highland coo paper like it had personally wronged her. She didn't see me at first. She saw the Book Bitches. Which, to be fair, is a lot to see.

"Absolutely not," she said, her instincts clearly on point. My mouth twitched. "Whatever it is."

"We haven't asked anything yet," Esther said, amused. "But since you're warmed up, why don't you come out and have a seat?"

Skye's gaze flicked to me then, sharp as flint. I held up my hands. *I am a hostage.* Her mouth pressed flat, and her head swiveled between the Book Bitches and Rosie and Harper.

Skye sighed and stormed past us, Rosie and Harper flanking her like charming bodyguards, and chose a seat by the fire. The Book Bitches arranged themselves opposite, a tribunal in knitwear. I took the far corner and tried to look like furniture.

Esther steepled her fingers. "Right. Business. Noah, if you intend to hide out in our town—"

"I'm not—"

"—and if we are to keep our mouths mostly shut about it—"

"That would be ideal, aye," I said.

"We don't work for free, dear," Meredith said. "We are community-minded. And the community is most emphatically *interested.*"

Shannon plopped a chunky tin on the table. It had a slot in the lid and the words *KINGSBARNS WINTER WARMER FUND* written in gold marker, slightly smudged. "So you'll buy our silence."

I blinked. "You're blackmailing me for charity."

"Precisely," Esther said. "It's called leverage for good. All proceeds go to the food bank, the library roof, and keeping the hall heated for the pensioners' dance. Also, we'd like nicer fairy lights for the green, but that's tier two."

Skye rubbed her temples. "You can't just shake him down."

"Oh, we can," Harper said cheerfully. "We're small business owners. We shake for a living."

Rosie nudged the tin toward me, smiling like she was selling me happiness in a jar. "Think of it as a community nondisclosure agreement. The more you help us with our Christmas fundraiser, the less we talk."

"And if I don't help?"

"Then we'll describe your jawline to the tabloids from memory," Rosie said, syrupy sweet. "We're very good with detail."

Skye made a strangled sound that I was choosing to believe was a laugh. "Leave him alone."

Esther's look softened when she turned to Skye, though her voice didn't. "Lass, you know we love you, which is why we're doing this. He needs a task, otherwise he's just going to be mooning about the inn bugging you. Which, from your emergency text message this morning begging us to get you out of there, *this* will get him out of your hair. The town needs the money. This is fate wrapped in glitter."

"I hate glitter," Skye muttered, but the fight had gone out of the line of her shoulders. She was also looking everywhere but me.

She wanted to get away from me? The thought saddened me, even though I could understand why. I'd been a first-rate arsehole to her, drunk on fame, and allowed Glen to produce the song he'd found written in my private notebook. While I'd been touring, making money, and enjoying its benefits, she'd been reminded over and over again that I'd used her for my own win. *Selfish, Byrne. Unforgivable, even if I'd not known how successful the song would be.*

"How much do you need? I could just transfer funds," I said, finally speaking.

"We accept." Cherise beamed at me.

"But that still doesn't keep you busy and isn't enough to buy our silence," Esther jumped in, glaring at Cherise.

I put my palms up. "Fine. What, exactly, are we talking about here?"

Six women and one bookstore owner leaned forward as one.

Harper tapped a marker on a sheet of paper. "Event ideas, go."

"Acoustic set," Shannon blurted. "Small. Intimate. Secret."

"Storytime with a rock star," Rosie said. "You read a romance book. We all fan ourselves and faint."

Skye rolled her eyes. I smiled. Even though I'd just met several of these women in the pub briefly last night, it had been enough to make quite the impression. Resistance was futile, it seemed.

"What? It's brainstorming." Rosie shrugged.

"Open mic but *you* have to be the judge," Meredith offered. "Also, you have to go last and blow everyone's socks off."

"Massage classes," Cherise suggested, then flushed when the women turned to look at her. "Sorry. That one escaped."

"A charity single," Esther said, eyes gleaming. "We'll call it *Kingsbarns at Christmas* and make the choir kids sing the chorus and release it on the internet."

"No," Skye said flatly.

"No to which?" Esther asked.

"All of it."

"Why?" Meredith asked, disappointed. "The tiny children in elf hats would be adorable."

Skye dragged in a breath and turned to Harper and Rosie, who were watching her expression closely. "Because he doesn't need more attention. Because I don't want this to become a circus. Because the last time a song got between us, it burned the house down."

Harper's eyes flicked to me. "We're newish," she said. "But we've heard … bits. Fill in the holes so we know which lines not to cross."

It was strangely merciful, the way she asked. Not hungry. Not nosy. Just … kind.

Skye stared at her hands, and I waited. Did she want me to tell them what happened? Did she want me to explain that I'd thought about her every day since she left me and wondered a thousand times if we could have somehow made it work? But then she spoke, and my heart broke again for the woman who I'd thought would be my forever.

She told them about the band making songs in a dusty garage, the manager who smelled like cigar smoke and new suits, the contract and the fight. She told them how she didn't trust Glen and I had, how she left to save herself from watching me choose everything but her. She told them how I wrote *Skye* and the world sang it and she got to be famous without asking and without pay.

She did not tell them about the kitchen floor we sat on after gigs, eating toast with jam because that's all we had money for. She didn't tell them the exact way her laugh sounded when I came up with a terrible rhyme. I didn't mention that I called twice and hung up both times because I was a coward, or that I drove past the inn at midnight and didn't stop, because apparently I preferred the worst version of myself.

I thought about saying those things, then I didn't, because this was her story. This was my penance. *And I needed to hear it. She's been hurt ... all because of me.*

Rosie slid a mug toward her. "That's ... a lot," she said softly.

"It is," Harper said. "But also"—she tilted her head at me—"he's here now."

Skye didn't look at me. "He's here to hide."

I wanted to protest but couldn't, because she wasn't entirely wrong. The scandal was a wave, and I was just a piece of driftwood caught on it.

Esther clapped her hands once, brisk. "Right. Feelings acknowledged. Back to fundraising."

Skye opened her mouth and then shut it, either out of exhaustion or because Harper put a hand on her arm. Rosie leaned into Skye's shoulder.

"Okay," I said, because sometimes the simplest route is through. "No press. No paparazzi. Nothing that puts a target on Skye or the inn. But I'll play the concert as long as we keep it small and very local."

Shannon squealed. Cherise clapped. Meredith made a noise that might have been a battle cry. Esther wrote *YES* on the paper in letters big enough to be seen from orbit.

"Venue," Harper said.

"Here," Rosie said immediately. "After hours. We shut the blinds and make hot chocolate and pretend the rest of the world is elsewhere."

"Too small," Cherise argued.

"Good call. The community center then?" Murmurs of agreement went up.

A book fell from a shelf at my side, causing me to jump,

and I leaned over to pick it up. Had I knocked the shelf? Turning the book over, I looked at the title.

What Women Really Want.

Annoyed, I put the book back on the shelf and tuned back into the conversation.

"We'll call it 'Cocoa & Carols,'" Shannon offered. "And then in tiny letters 'and a very quiet acoustic set by a guest.'"

"Or we say 'John Smith Live,'" Harper suggested, deadpan.

"Oh, he *is* my favorite artist," I said, smiling.

Esther ticked boxes. "Tickets?"

"Tickets first. Donation at the door on the day if tickets haven't sold out," Cherise said. "Pay what you can."

"Security," Meredith said, very serious. "Gregory on the door. He can glower."

I'd seen Gregory. He was not typically who I'd enlist for security services, but this was their gig now.

"Program," Rosie said. "We'll lead carols for twenty minutes, then the kiddos' choir, then our guest, and then more carols so we don't let him be the last thing people hear —no offense—and then biscuits."

"Set list," Esther said, pivoting to me like a general. "No heartbreak ballads that name names."

"Deal."

Skye's head came up at that. Her eyes met mine, surprised.

"I'll do a couple of old Christmas songs," I said. "Ones everyone knows. And one new thing that won't get me sued or anyone hurt."

"Right," Harper said, clapping her hands now. "Assignments. Rosie and I will handle poster design and cocoa.

Cherise, you're on donations. Meredith, biscuits with those little icings only you can make. And get the Two Sisters Bakery on the rest. Shannon, choir wrangling. Esther, crowd control."

Rosie tapped a pen on her lip. "Costumes?"

"No," Skye and I said at the same time.

"Matching scarves then," Rosie said, untroubled. "Tasteful. Coordinated."

"Rosie," Harper warned.

"Fine." Rosie sighed. "But I'm buying cinnamon sticks for the cocoa and nobody can stop me."

The bell at the front rang. Rosie jumped up, the Book Bitches flowed after her in a tide of wool and cheer, already dictating who would stand where and whether there would be glitter.

Skye stayed seated. Harper squeezed her hand and patted my shoulder as she passed me. When it was just the two of us, the room shrank to the size of a heart.

"You don't owe them anything," she said, eyes on the paper, voice tight. "You don't owe anyone anything."

"I owe a lot of things," I said. "Maybe not this. But it feels like a start."

She looked at me then. Not through me. *At* me. I had to resist the impulse to put my hands in my pockets like a teenager.

"You're not allowed to be charming," she said.

"I'm terrible at being charming," I said. "Ask anyone. I'm surly for sport."

Her mouth twitched despite herself. "You always were better onstage."

"Thanks?" I raised an eyebrow.

"That wasn't a compliment," she said, but her voice had softened a shade.

"Right." I blew out a breath. "Look, I'll keep my head down. I'll play the fundraiser and work on not being a walking PR disaster. I'll ... just stay out of your way."

She frowned. "You don't have to stay *out* of my way. You live down the hall."

On the table, the donation tin gleamed. I took my wallet out and slid notes through the slot.

"Thank you," she said.

"Buy extra cinnamon sticks," I said.

Her laugh was quick and surprised. God, I'd missed that sound.

"Go on then," she said, shooing me with two fingers. "Before Esther recruits you to dress as a shepherd for the nativity."

"I'd be a terrible shepherd," I said, backing toward the door. "I'm emotionally unreliable."

"True," she said solemnly. "And sheep can tell."

Banter. For the first time in years, there had been banter between Skye and me. How crazy that my heart felt somewhat lighter from something so simple.

I spent the afternoon being useful in ways that didn't require my name. Gregory had me carry boxes of donations for the families in need to be packed and wrapped at the bookshop. I fixed a string of fairy lights with electrical tape and a prayer. Cherise made me fold raffle tickets while she told me stories about how the village used to be when she was a girl. Meredith handed me a biscuit and said, "Eat, you look like you're about to waste away."

I'd lost a little weight after the last tour and due to

recent stress, but I was by no means thin. The women just seemed to like to feed me at all times. It was comforting, reminding me of my own mum, who was currently enjoying three months in Australia ever since she and my dad had retired and decided to chase the sun. I happily funded their travels, and nothing gave me more joy than the random pictures I'd get from places all over the world, usually of my dad showing me a fancy new toilet feature he'd just discovered in far-flung places like Japan.

Everywhere I went, people gave me a look that said they recognized me but had been briefed on the rules. Nobody asked for a photo. Nobody said *Skye*. Nobody made me into a headline.

And ... I realized that I liked helping out with random tasks.

It was the most useful I'd felt in a while.

When you become famous, you stop doing things for yourself. Not that I minded handing off some chores, like cleaning and laundry, to a maid service. But it was the little things, like driving my own car, getting myself a cup of coffee, that kind of thing ... that I'd missed out on. Once Kingsbarns got the word to leave me alone—the Book Bitches gossip network moved faster than lightning—I was free to move about in relative ease.

And I found it refreshing, really, *really* refreshing.

Maybe I'd been burned out for a while now, but there was something about sitting down and helping with a basic task like working on signs for a Christmas concert that was refilling my well in ways that I couldn't quite explain.

It didn't hurt that it gave me close proximity to Skye, even though she still largely avoided conversation with me.

Still, every once in a while, I'd catch her looking at me, her eyes unreadable, and she'd quickly look away.

My first love.

It was hard not to beat myself up for past choices when I was back seeing her every day. What if ... there were so many *what ifs* running through my head.

I'd been young and stupid. I'd let my pride get in the way of our love, focusing on the record contract instead of building together with Skye. She'd been right. Even then. Our music was good enough that it wouldn't have been our only chance for success.

When I'd learned she'd married a few years after our breakup, I'd hit the bottle pretty hard, and my angstiest album ever had been born. My heartbreak had earned me a lot of money, and later, when I'd heard about her divorce, my most fun and lighthearted album had followed. Whether I liked it or not, Skye had been a part of my music since day one. She was the pillar holding up my career, and even though I'd been the one to take an axe to it, I couldn't help but hold some hope that one day she'd let me back in.

Even if just as a friend—though every ounce of me wanted more. I hadn't known that before coming here, and yet, admitting that thought to myself made me realize I'd known it all along. It was ridiculous, sometimes, the games we played with ourselves. Maybe it was too much to hope that Skye would let me back into her life again, but we were both here, now, in this moment together.

So all I could do was try.

Five

SKYE

There are few betrayals more personal than a shower that lies to you.

I turned the hot tap and waited. The pipes coughed. The boiler whirred. I stuck a hopeful hand under the spray and was rewarded with a blast of Arctic punishment that made my soul leave my body and hover near the ceiling, filing a complaint.

"Traitor," I told the shower. It hissed in what I took as agreement.

Lovely. Now I needed to fix this before the guests started complaining. Dreading having to call the annoying plumber, I wrapped myself in my robe, shoved my feet into slipper-socks with pom-poms that had seen better days, and went downstairs. I'd barely hit the last step when I heard the metallic clank of tools, a muffled curse, and the suspiciously alive rattle of my ancient hot-water heater.

I rounded the corner to the utility cupboard, ready to tell off a burglar with hopefully excellent DIY skills, and stopped so hard my slippers squeaked.

Noah was kneeling on the floor with the cupboard door open and his shoulders inside like he intended to climb into Narnia via the boiler. His jacket was on the floor, sleeves were shoved up, and his forearms flexed around a tool I did not know the name of, which felt like a personal failing and kind of annoyed me. There were two safety manuals open on the floor, neither of which he seemed to be reading, and the muscles in his arms flexed.

It would be rude of me to ogle him while he was working, but apparently it was too early in the morning for me to remember my manners, and I took a moment to appreciate his very fine backside. I used to wrap my hands around his waist and dig my palms into the back seat of his jeans, loving how he felt beneath my hands.

"What are you doing?" I asked, which came out more sharply than I intended because I was cold and the morning had already betrayed me and also it hurt to think of sexy moments from the past with him.

He startled, bumped his head, and swore in a tone that even would have made the Book Bitches scold him.

"Good morning," he said, backing out of the cupboard, big and awkward and annoyingly handsome, into my hallway. "I'm negotiating with your hot-water heater."

"Oh good," I said. "Because it's been very stubborn lately and has refused all my reasonable offers. Have you tried threatening it with a sledgehammer?"

"Step one on my list," he said, wiping his hand on his shirt. "Step two is asking it nicely with a spanner. Step three is calling Gregory. He seems to know all the right people to fix things in town."

"You can't just … fix things," I said, flailing my hands. "That's not … that's not how we do this."

"We?" He tilted his head and I flushed.

"I mean. Here. At the inn," I said, waving at the cupboard. "I have a system."

"It appears your system is failing," he said mildly, and the worst thing was he wasn't wrong. It was embarrassing to have him see the worn edges of my struggling business.

"Why are you in my cupboard, Noah?"

"I couldn't sleep. Your pipes sounded like a rave in a tin can. There's a leak right there." He pointed, and I had to edge closer to see, which meant I had to smell him. Coffee and soap and a hint of cocoa. The nerve. "It's dripping onto the pilot, which means it's struggling to stay lit."

He touched something with the spanner, the boiler sighed, then caught, then purred in a way I haven't heard in months.

I let myself have one, just one, tiny groan of pleasure. Hot water might be my love language.

"Don't," I said quickly, catching his grin. "Don't look smug."

"I wouldn't dream of it." Still … the corners of his lips tugged up in that deliciously handsome face.

He was absolutely dreaming of it.

"I appreciate the … help," I said, because my gran had trained me to use manners. "But you can't just start fixing things around here."

He sat back on his heels. "Why not?"

"Because." I folded my arms over my robe so my annoyance had a shelf to perch on. "Because it's *my* job."

"And you're doing three people's worth of work by yourself."

"It's my inn."

"And it was your gran's inn," he said, not unkindly. "And she'd haunt you for letting this place chew you up."

The words landed like an elbow to the ribs. "Leave my gran out of this."

"I'm offering help."

"You're offering control," I snapped, surprising both of us. "You always do. You swoop in and decide how the story goes and everyone else is supposed to clap and say thank you."

His jaw tightened. "That's not fair."

"No? That manager I told you not to trust. Remember him? You put your life in his hands and drove away while I stood on the footpath with a suitcase and a backbone and promised myself I'd survive it. Forgive me if watching you crouch in my cupboard with a spanner feels like déjà vu in a cheaper jacket."

He flinched. I hated that it made me feel vindicated.

"I'm not trying to rewrite history," he said evenly. "I'm trying to fix a leak."

"Beautiful metaphor. Very on brand."

"Skye." He put the spanner down and lifted his hands like I might bite him. "You're tired. Let me take some weight. I can do repairs, I can run out for supplies, and I can even answer the bloody phone. I grew up here too, remember? I know my way around a tool shed. I'm not ... helpless."

"And I'm not helpless either."

"I never said you were."

"You didn't have to." My voice went sharp. "Every time you 'help,' I hear, 'You can't handle this.'"

"That's not what I mean."

"Well, that's what I hear!"

"Skye. I love ... I mean, *loved*, you." Noah's voice caught and my eyes widened. Had he just said what I thought he'd said? "Despite what you may think, you still matter to me. I know I have a lot of sins to atone for, and if sorting your hot-water heater out is a place to start, well, I'd like to. I want to ..." His voice trailed off, and what looked like longing filled his eyes.

I had no idea how to respond to that. All reasonable thought left my brain as I stared at his mouth, wanting desperately to feel his kiss. Just once more.

We stared at each other, breath fogging in the cold hall, the boiler purring like a cat that enjoyed drama.

He'll be gone soon, Skye, and then life will return to normal. My thoughts returned, waving red flags at me.

Footsteps creaked on the stairs. One of my American guests, a nice woman in her sixties having a tour of Scotland, called down to me. "Skye, dear, have you got any more of that marmalade? I'm afraid I've gone through it all."

I took a shaky breath. "I have guests. I have rooms to turn over. I have a boiler that, thank you, is no longer plotting my demise. I don't have bandwidth for ... for you in my cupboards and whatever else this is."

"Copy that." A muscle in his cheek jumped. He

opened his mouth to say something else, but coward that I was, I turned my back and fled to my room and quickly got ready for the day, before racing to the kitchen. My hands shook as I set up trays, the cups clinking in an accusatory way, as if they'd been following along and had notes.

By the time the tea was poured, Noah had vanished. His jacket was gone and so was the spanner. The boiler, that traitor, continued to hum.

I carried the tray into the lounge, delivered tea to the guests, smiled, joked, lied charmingly, and escaped back into the hall where nobody could see me crack.

The house breathed around me. The inn had lungs ... anyone who said otherwise hadn't slept in an old building long enough. Too wound up to do the laundry, I went upstairs and locked the door to my flat. I just needed a moment to sort my thoughts out.

"I love ... I mean, loved, you."

I couldn't ignore how my heart had instantly responded to his words, and a part of me hated myself for how excited I'd been to hear he actually still cared. Or *had* cared. Or at the very least, wanted to make some amends. What had he meant by that?

Leaning my forehead against the door, I took several deep breaths and tried to get some control of my emotions. During check-ins, I was professional, competent, and mildly amused by the chaos of human behavior. When things went wrong, I never stressed. I just got things done. Why had Noah's arrival turned me into someone who nearly cried at a boiler and a banshee who yelled at a man for helping? I wasn't someone who normally had wild swings of emotion, and now I felt untethered, and unsure of my footing.

I paced the tiny sitting room.

The radiator clicked. A gust of winter wind rattled the window. The air shifted.

And then my gran—dead eight years and still very much herself—cleared her throat.

"Are you done?" she asked.

My head snapped up so fast my neck made a noise. She stood by the fireplace as if she'd come out of it like Santa, in her house cardigan and her sensible skirt and her leather slippers with the little bow. She gave me the look she reserved for people who left wet towels on floors.

"You're not real," I told her, my chest hitching, because apparently my response to ghosts is impoliteness.

"Och, I am," she said. "And don't you be sassing me."

"Bloody hell. But I must be stressed. *This* has to be a stress response." I flapped a hand toward her. "Lack of sleep. A byproduct of being emotionally waterboarded by a man with a spanner."

"Language," she said mildly, which was rich coming from someone who once told a plumber to stop "faffin" about like a damp hen.

I pressed my palms to my eyes. "I am hallucinating my gran."

"You're avoiding the point," she said, and crossed to sit in her chair. "You were always good at that, pet."

"I am very busy," I announced, unsure of what to say. "I have rooms to turn over."

"You have a heart to unclench," she said, like she was reading the menu and ordering for me. "Sit."

I sat at her feet, wanting closeness, because, even if this was a stress-induced hallucination, I still missed her.

Up close, she wasn't ... see-through like I thought a ghost would be. She wasn't a wisp. She was my gran as I remembered her. Softly weathered skin, eyes like bluebells, wrinkled hands that had done a lifetime of useful things. The only thing that betrayed the impossible was the way the air around her shivered and brightened.

"You're not real," I tried again, softer.

"I'll always be real, lass," she said, and then more softly, "your love keeps it so."

I swallowed, tears pricking my eyes, and laid my cheek on the cushion next to her. For a moment, it felt like a light puff of air blew my hair back, as though she once again stroked my hair like she used to when I was a child.

"Why are you here? Now?" I'd silently asked for her help a hundred times through the years, and she'd never once shown me anything. But here she was, on a day that my emotions were unraveling like someone tossing a ball of yarn down the stairs.

"Because I think you need someone to be honest with."

"Noah was in the cupboard and he shouldn't have been," I said, somewhat inanely, but knowing she'd understand about how odd it felt to find a guest in a non-guest space of the house.

"I saw. He looked very nice while he was in the cupboard."

"Gran." I rolled my eyes.

"Don't roll your eyes at me. You can put a front on for everyone else. But I can see right through you, Skye, dear."

"I can't let him in again."

"And why ever not? People change. There's a lifetime of learning between who you both were then and who you are now."

Heat crawled up my neck. "He left. I told him that bloody manager would eat him alive, and he left anyway. He wrote a song and sold my name to the entire planet."

"You told him your truth," she said. "Good. And then you told yourself a story so sharp you could live inside it and not feel anything else."

"That's very poetic for a hallucination."

"Skye Kerrigan," she said, and my name in her mouth made me ten and thirty-seven at once. "Do not let history repeat itself because it's easier than risking joy."

I squeezed my eyes shut. "I'm not repeating anything. I'm avoiding potholes."

"You're avoiding love."

"I'm not ... he's not ..." I flailed uselessly. *Why was my hallucination of Gran discussing love and Noah in the same breath?*

Noah wasn't here because he still loved me. That ship sailed long ago. She was confused with a fairy tale.

"Gran, Noah is a man who has a complicated relationship with commitment and publicity and his own hair. I am an innkeeper with a budget spreadsheet that could make saints weep. This is not a fairy tale."

"You are allowed to still love him and to also be angry. You are allowed to need help and also be capable."

"Is this on a tea towel somewhere?" I muttered.

She ignored me. "That boy broke his own heart when he left. Yours too. You both did what you thought kept you safe. And now you stand here with your eyes clenched so tight you can't even see the second chance the universe is handing you."

I sucked in a breath. Did Noah and I really have a second chance at love? The thought was so wild and untested, and yet, it surfaced from the hidden recesses of my heart like a submerged buoy floating for the surface.

"The only thing that matters," she said, and her voice went low like a secret, "is love."

I bristled. "That's easy to say when it's not your heart on the line."

"I have very few regrets, Skye. Not telling your granddad about the day I decided to keep the inn even though we'd have to take out a loan? That was a regret—brief. He forgave me before I finished the sentence. Not taking the trip to Greece when the girls were small? I thought we didn't have the money. We had enough. We would have found it. And the last ... is every time I watched you use stubbornness where tenderness would have done the job and didn't push you to relent."

Tears pricked hot. "I'm not stubborn."

She raised one white brow. "You are a granite wall in a pretty dress." She looked sadly at my worn trousers. "When you wear a dress, that is."

"I can't let him come in here and push me around," I said, still hung up on my hurt.

"No one said you had to," she said. "And he's hardly pushing, is he? He's helping. Let him in the door. Keep your keys in your pocket. That's called love, not surrender."

"I don't know how to do that." The word "love" in the same breath as Noah felt shimmery and shaky, like something as ephemeral as my gran sitting in the chair talking to me.

"You learn," she said simply. "You learn by doing."

Silence fell in a soft layer. Downstairs, a phone rang, someone laughed, and the boiler hummed, loyal now that it had received attention.

I wiped at my face with the heel of my hand like a teenager. "If you're not real," I said, defeated, "you might be here because I'm edging toward a breakdown."

She smiled, brief and pleased. "Or you might be edging toward a breakthrough."

"I hate that more."

"I know."

"I miss you," I said, and the truth of it loosened something braided too tight inside my ribs.

"I miss you too," she said, and for a breath she shimmered, went bright as a swallowed candle, and I thought I'd imagined all of it. Then she was Gran again, solid as the chair, stern as the cold.

"Are you going to haunt him?" I asked, because if my brain was inventing cinema, I wanted bonus features.

"I'll haunt whoever needs it," she said. "Today that's you."

"Thanks," I said dryly. "Terrific."

She laughed and it was my favorite sound, the one that says she thinks I'm ridiculous and precious in equal measure. Then she sobered. "Love is the only thing that matters. Not the song. Not your pride. Not the fear. If it comes to your door and asks to help carry the groceries, you let it. You can always say no to the cooking later."

"That metaphor fell apart at the end," I said.

"My metaphors always did need a bit of glue," she said fondly, and stood, smoothing her skirt. "I'll be off then."

"Where?" I asked, suddenly desperate to keep her with me.

She looked toward the window, as if the wind had sent a note. "Wherever I'm needed." She leaned down, cupped my face, and I felt the softest brush of air at my cheeks. "Eat a proper lunch. You get mean when you're hungry. And tell that boy to fix the radiator in the blue room as it wheezes like a sick accordion."

And she was gone.

The air sagged, and the cushion sprang back.

I sat very still, astounded at what had just occurred.

"Stress," I said aloud. "Pure stress."

The radiator in the blue room wheezed like a sick accordion. I could hear it all the way from here.

"Fine," I told the universe. Shaking, I stood, and looked out the window, wondering if I'd see my gran sailing away toward the ocean like Mary Poppins with her umbrella. Instead, a moody winter sky met my gaze, and I turned, pulling the feeling of Gran being close once again to my heart.

I washed my face in the tiny bathroom sink, pinched color into my cheeks like a Victorian ghost, and marched downstairs with intent.

Noah was in the hall, jacket on, as if he'd correctly deduced that he should stay away from me. He looked up when he heard me. Something moved through his face before wariness settled on his expression. Bloody man.

"Before you run away to do ... whatever it is you do when you pretend you don't care," I said, and his mouth quirked, "the radiator in the blue room wheezes. It sounds like it's dying. See what you can do."

He blinked. "Yes, boss."

"And"—the word stuck. I forced it through—"thank you. For the boiler."

He lifted a shoulder, shrugging off my thanks. "Anytime. Um, there's a hardware shop in Crail that I can pick up a few things to patch some problem areas I've noted around here. I'll be back before lunch. If that's okay?"

It took everything in my power not to tell him "no" but since I was still reeling from a surprise ghost visit from my gran and had nobody to talk to about it, I relented.

"I'd appreciate that," I said, remembering that Gran was probably watching and railing at me to be *nice* to the handsome man.

"Great. I'll be back shortly." He saluted, ridiculously so, and left.

The hall felt bigger without him and worse. Needing a diversion, and time to think about the visit from Gran, I made scones, the kind she'd taught me—the cold butter rubbed in until the flour looked like wet sand, the milk splashed just enough, the dough patted, not bullied. I set a timer and chopped fruit for compote and told myself sternly that I had not seen a ghost and that if I had, nobody would believe me anyway.

Esther texted me.

> I heard your boiler was on the fritz. Do you need my help?

. . .

How had she heard that already? I briefly wondered if my gran visited her as well.

> What do you know about fixing boilers?

> My hubby knows a thing or two about heating things up.

> Gah! No. I'm good. It's fixed.

> Ahhh, you let Noah fix it, didn't you?
> That's practically a betrothal in this town.
> Have you shagged him yet?

> Esther!

> What? Best to test the milk before you buy the cow, dear.

. . .

Please go menace someone else.

Can't. Being menacing is too much cardio. But I'm proud of you, dear.

I put the phone down and pretended my eyes didn't sting.

The timer dinged. I pulled scones from the oven, split one open, and ate it too hot, butter melting down my fingers, because carbs—*and fat*—were needed.

When Noah came back, arms full of bags of tools and hardware supplies, I did not smile.

But I didn't run, either.

That felt like progress Gran would approve of.

Six

NOAH

I came down late that night, after a particularly long nap, because I was still wrestling with jet lag. The inn had the gentle quiet that isn't silence—old-house quiet, radiators ticking and the walls settling and sighing. I followed the warmth to the lounge and stopped in the doorway.

Skye was decorating the tree by herself.

It wasn't a grand tree—nothing that screamed hotel lobby It was a stubborn, well-meaning Scots pine that looked like it had picked its way home across the fields. She'd dragged it into the corner near the hearth and strung the bottom half in lights while the other half waited like an unlit promise. There was a plastic tub of ornaments open on the rug, a tangle of paper chains she'd clearly made by hand, and a mug steamed at her elbow. The fire threw copper into her hair, and she'd kicked off her shoes and wore those socks with little pom-poms at the ankles.

And she was singing.

Not loud. Not performing. Just the soft, automatic singing you do when your hands are busy and you forget anyone could be listening—low and warm and a little husky where the day had sanded it down. It was a song I didn't know, which annoyed me in a petty way because I used to know all her songs.

You can spend years pretending you don't remember the precise temperature of someone's voice, and then one note finds the tuning fork in your ribs and everything you've built shivers on its foundation. I leaned on the doorframe and let it happen because some mistakes you have to witness to fix.

She looked up at the shift of light. Saw me. The song cut off with a swallow.

"You missed tea," she said. Which in Skye language meant how much of that did you hear?

"Couldn't sleep last night, and I slept too long now." I held up hands. "I heard you fighting a losing battle with a string of lights and thought I'd offer diplomatic assistance."

"They're feral," she said, deadpan. "They came out of the box as a knot with a superiority complex."

"Hand them over, then."

"It's your funeral," she warned, but she passed me the snarled knot anyway.

Up close she smelled like lemon and sugar. She'd gotten glitter on her cheekbone, traitorous stuff that has the survival instincts of a cockroach. I had the sudden, stupid urge to lick it off her face and had to move backward to avoid becoming a headline.

I took the lights to the hearth rug and started the ritual —free a loop, swear, roll, pass under, curse again. In the meantime, Skye slowly dug through a box of ornaments, unwrapping each one and holding it in front of her for a moment.

"You're humming," I said after a minute, because I like to make my own trouble. "You always hum when you're nervous."

"I always hum when I'm working," she corrected. "It keeps the ghosts from making suggestions."

"Your gran thanked me for fixing the radiator in the blue room," I said before I could stop my mouth.

One of the reasons I'd woken so suddenly from my nap was that I'd sensed a presence in my room. Even now, I still wasn't sure if I'd been dreaming or awake. When I'd slitted my eyes open, Skye's gran had been in the corner in a sliver of light and had offered me thanks. She'd also told me not to give up on her granddaughter before she'd winked out of sight. I'd closed my eyes again, my heart hammering, and now I was only partially certain it had just been a dream.

She paused. "Did she, now?"

"She's very persuasive."

"That's a nice way to phrase it," she said, but the edge of a smile had snuck up on her mouth. "I thought I saw her as well, but I put it down to stress."

My eyebrows drew up.

Had we really been visited by a ghost? But Skye's smile was pained, and the lines on her forehead tight, and I didn't want to make a big deal about it if she wasn't comfortable discussing it more deeply.

"That's fair. I was probably still dreaming." I glanced over at her, trying to judge her mood. "It was nice to see her, even if it was just a dream. Do you miss her?"

"Aye." Skye shrugged but offered nothing else. Perhaps it was too much to hope that she'd share more of her life with me.

"The radiator still sounds like an asthmatic accordion, by the way. I'll have another go in the morning. I picked up more keys at the store."

"Thank you," she said, quietly and real in a way that made me feel unsteady.

I freed the last loop. Held up the lights like a fish I'd just caught. "Victory."

"You've got glitter on your face," she said, amused.

"You've got glitter on your soul," I said and then when her mouth rounded, I immediately felt awkward for what I'd just said. Had that been too romantic? Too complimentary? Navigating conversations with Skye right now made me feel like I was picking my way through a minefield.

"Come on, let's test these."

Skye bent and plugged the lights in and they blinked obediently, warm and soft. She made a small, pleased noise she probably didn't know she made, and my stupid heart obligingly fell down a flight of stairs.

She used to make that pleased noise in bed with me, after making love, and right before she drifted off to sleep. I wanted her to make that sound for me again.

Instead, I stood, and we strung the lights together, doing that instinctive dance two people do when their bodies remember being a team. Soon enough, the tree was well lit, and I stood back, pleased with our work.

"Star or angel?" I asked.

"Gran liked the star," she said, digging in the box, then surfaced with a brass ornament that had been polished within an inch of its life. "It's older than I am, I think."

"Up you go, then."

I held the chair while she set the star, doing my best to not admire her bum that was dangerously close to my face.

Who was I kidding? I was one hundred percent admiring her bum. I wanted to lean in and bite it, but that would likely get me a swat to the head or her tumbling off the chair.

"Not bad," I said, admiring our work so far.

"Ornaments now," she said briskly, and crouched by the box. "These are the good ones. Don't manhandle them. If you break an heirloom, my gran will haunt you."

"I honestly don't know if that's a joke or not," I said, and sat on the rug with her because it felt cozy. I needed some cozy in my life.

She held up a glass bauble with a crack running through it like a tiny lightning bolt. "This one's from when I was six and thought glitter glue could repair anything."

"Was it a wrong assumption?"

"Glitter glue repairs nothing and resides everywhere," she said. "Like hope. Or mold."

I took a tiny wooden stag ornament and held it up. "We had one like this in my mum's box. Remember how she'd invite everyone over for decorating the Christmas tree?" I asked, and then immediately hated myself for throwing the past into the room like a lit match. Skye had lost her parents young, when she'd been just a baby, and most in Kingsbarns had collectively joined to help her grandparents raise her, my parents included.

But Skye didn't flinch.

"Your mum used to come to the carols, too," she said, softly. "She stood at the back and sang like she didn't want to, and then on the last verse gave it her all."

"Sounds like her."

"She used to plait my hair in the school yard when my gran was too busy."

"She told me once you had more patience than I did," I said. "I've been thinking about that every time you untangle some tinsel."

She looked down into the box. "Untangling is not the same as fixing."

"It's a start."

Our eyes met over the box, and I wanted more than anything to reach out, to pull her close, and to see if we still could sing the same harmony together. Instead, I bent my head and pulled out another ornament and handed it to Skye.

We laughed over the ornaments as Skye hung them. A crocheted bell that had seen love and dust. A paper angel whose head was taped on. A unicorn I'd have bet a month's wages came from the pub. A star shaped from foil sweet wrappers, a faded tartan bow. None of it matched. All of it was exactly right.

She hummed again, and I found myself sliding under her melody out of muscle memory, not loud, just there. Harmony was a trust fall. Before, she would have leaned into it without thinking. Now she stilled, then let it happen. The knot between my ribs loosened enough to breathe.

"You remember the Glasgow garage?" she asked.

"Which one?"

"The one where we rehearsed the week before the Dumfries gig. You left the amp at home because you were sure you could 'coax tone' out of the room."

"It was a very tonal room."

"It was a damp cave that smelled like cabbage."

"You wrote the bridge to *Five a.m.* on the floor with your foot tapping in those worn Doc Martens," I said, the memory unfolding itself. "We kept the foot tap in the demo. You can hear it if you know where to listen."

"First time we figured out we could fight without breaking the song," she said. "Second time was that pub in Perth. The one with the carpet that made everyone's feet stick."

" 'Stickier than sin,'" I recited, because her gran had said it once and we'd used it in a song. "You sang like the ceiling was listening."

"The ceiling was listening because it was falling," she said, and the smile she gave me then belonged to the girl who once dared me to busk a busy farmers market on a warm summer morning in July.

We hung in easy silence for a few minutes, putting the finishing touches on the tree.

"Do you still write?" I asked the question that had been burning the back of my tongue since I'd walked in and she'd broken me open with a hum.

She fiddled with an ornament of a dove as if it had suddenly become very interesting. "I write lists."

"Skye."

"I run an inn," she said, which was not an answer, and we both knew it.

"You run an inn and what else?"

"And," she admitted, quietly, "sometimes I write ... bits. Lines. The middle of a thing that doesn't exist yet."

"Bring them to a beginning," I said gently. "Or an end."

"I don't know if I want ends," she said, even quieter.

"Try a chorus, then." I was dying to reach out and brush a loose strand of her hair back, so I put a hand on the box to keep from touching her. "You taught me how to finish things, you know."

"I taught you how to finish things you liked," she amended. "I wouldn't take credit for your tax filings."

"Too soon," I said, holding my hands to my gut like I was wounded, and the joke did the job of turning us back toward light.

"I'm sorry," I said, because the quiet had settled into a shape that could hold it.

"For what?" she asked, meeting my eyes, her chin lifted.

"For making the past a song and leaving you to live in the echo."

Skye sucked in her breath and stilled.

"Thank you," Skye finally said, and a weight I'd carried for years lessened slightly. "I needed to hear that. You hurt me, Noah. It was my choice to leave, and I take responsibility for that, but the song ... och. That was tough to stomach."

"I'm sorry for it," I said, meaning it.

"You shouldn't be." Skye surprised me with her words, and from the look on her face, had surprised herself as well.

"It's a damn good song. Music should be honest. Yours was. It didn't mean it didn't hurt, but it was still a great song."

"I hate that I hurt you," I whispered.

Skye swallowed and looked away. "Cocoa?" she asked, surprising me. "Rosie sent me home with extra cinnamon sticks."

"I have never said no to cocoa," I said, taking the olive branch.

Without thinking about it, I followed her to the kitchen. We moved around each other like muscle memory —she rummaged for mugs, I found the good cocoa tin behind the box of tea. While the milk warmed, she hummed again, and I crept into the harmony like a thief who only steals back what he gave away.

Skye caught herself, and stopped, glancing shyly at me.

"You should sing more," I encouraged, not wanting to break the mood that strung between us.

"I do," she said, defensive. "In my kitchen. To my kettle."

"Your kettle is very lucky."

When I handed her the mug, our fingers touched, and I jolted, her nearness having me on edge.

"Careful," she said softly. "It's hot."

"It always has been," I said and Skye slanted me a look.

We took our drinks back to the lounge, sat on the rug with our backs against the sofa so we could admire the tree. Silence stretched out between us, but it wasn't uncompanionable.

It was nice, in fact. To just sit together.

My phone buzzed.

Just once. Just a small, mosquito hum against my thigh.

I ignored it.

It buzzed again, insistent, then again, and then it started the full-on vibration that says *you'll want to pretend you didn't see this, but you will, and it will make everything harder.*

Skye didn't look at me, but the line of her spine changed. I pulled the phone out.

The screen was a wall of messages.

Texts from bandmates—two words, my name, a curse.

Mate, turn on the news.

They raided his office.

Call me NOW.

You're screwed.

My thumb found a link in my agent's message before my brain could read it. The video loaded, the volume down, captions scuddling across the bottom.

BREAKING: Manager of chart-topping band under

investigation for fraud, embezzlement; HMRC and police execute warrants; assets frozen; sources say millions missing; artists blindsided. Developing story.

The thumbnail was Glen's face. The man I'd put between me and good sense for over a decade. Walking fast under a gray sky, coat too thin for winter. Behind him, someone held a box of folders. A hand reached into the frame with a mic and his eyes flashed something mean and small.

My skin went cold and hot at the same time.

"Don't," Skye said beside me, and I realized that I didn't know what to do.

It was the first time in a really long time that I didn't know my way forward.

Panic tightened my throat. Anger burned my core.

"I need to—" *What?* I didn't know what came after need.

She set her cocoa down carefully.

"Look at me," she said.

I looked.

"You didn't do this," she said, her voice direct. "You *didn't*. You were stupid, and loyal, and terrified to admit you'd hitched yourself to someone who would throw you to the wolves. But you didn't do this."

"I signed the papers," I said. "I played by his rules."

"You trusted the wrong person," she said. "That's not a crime. It's a bruise."

"I'm going to be dragged into it."

"Aye, you will."

"It'll crawl over everything. Over you. I'm doing this to you. Again."

That might have been the worst thing of it all. Once more, Skye would get her name dragged into the spotlight because of me. *Why had I come here, bringing this to her doorstep? What had I been thinking?*

"So we deal." Skye looked up at me, a determined glint in her eyes. "Gran always told me to just crack on with things when life got tough. And I'll take her advice here. With you. There's not a thing to be done about the fact that you're here, now, and scandal is breaking over your head. So we deal with it."

"How?" I sounded more childish than I wanted to admit, but not for the first time, I was staring at the consequences of my fame.

"New house rules," she said immediately. "Curtains down. You don't open the front door. You don't answer numbers you don't know. You don't go anywhere alone. If the paps come here, we call Esther and the Book Bitches, and they'll do that thing where they become a wall made of ridiculous Christmas jumpers and moral outrage."

"I don't want to put you in it. Or any of them in it." Though the Book Bitches were terrifying, they didn't know what the paparazzi could be like.

"You don't get to decide whether I'm in it," she said, and my breath caught. *There was my girl. My wildfire.* "You brought the storm, but I own a roof. That's how this works."

I laughed, surprised, but beyond grateful. "I don't deserve you."

"Correct," she said, because even Skye could be merciful in odd ways. "But you have me for the moment."

My heart shifted in my chest. Hearing those words ... "you have me" made my entire body heat with longing.

My phone buzzed again.

"Drink your hot chocolate," she said. "Then go upstairs and pack a bag in case we need to move you to the flat above the pub for a day or two. It has good locks. I'll text Harper just in case. Esther will put the pensioners on the lookout. We'll draw the curtains here and you'll wear your hat pulled low."

"You're good at this," I said, surprised. I'd had years of ducking from cameras, but she hadn't. Not like this.

Skye smiled, my compliment warming her face.

We sat a long minute with the awful news glow lighting my palm.

She leaned back against the sofa and closed her eyes. "For what it's worth," she murmured. "I never wanted to be right about him."

"I know you didn't. I should have known that. Back then." I said, and put my hand, palm up, on the floor between us like you hold out a treat to a stray, scared dog. After a heartbeat, she set her fingers in mine. Light. Not a promise. But, enough. For now.

"Up," she said, after our palms had warmed against each other. "Pack. Then sleep if you can. Tomorrow you'll need your voice to say the right things or nothing at all."

"What if I don't know the right things to say?"

"Then say nothing," she said. "And let the people who love you be loud."

My heart hiccupped at the word *love*, but I couldn't bring myself to comment on it. The olive branch between us was too new, too frail, to test its weight on something heavier.

Instead, I did something I'd been wanting to for years. I hugged her, briefly, but when she leaned into me and looped her arms around my waist, it felt like, for a moment, that nothing else in the world mattered but us. *And that I could face the coming storm ... because I wasn't alone.*

Seven

SKYE

There's a uniquely Scottish silence that isn't silence at all—just the wind holding its breath and the sea deciding whether to kick up a fuss or not. We didn't have that this morning.

We had vans.

We had cameras.

We had men in black parkas practicing their "I'm just doing my job" faces.

The paparazzi had arrived.

By the time I made it downstairs, the lane outside the inn looked like the king was about to visit. Five cars nose-to-tail, a tripod in my herb bed, a man in a yellow hi-vis vest that definitely did not come from anywhere official. And between them and my front gate stood Esther and the Book

Bitches, wearing knitwear and righteous purpose like armor.

I cracked the side door and peered out, biting back a grin as Esther stomped forward, the poor paps ready to fight a battle none of them realized they'd already lost.

"Parking is residents-only, lads," Esther announced, hands on hips, clipboard at the ready. She had added a high-visibility sash over her coat, which I suspected she'd made out of pure audacity.

One of the photographers held up his press pass. "We're working press."

"Aye, and I'm the Queen of Sheba," Esther said. "Thirty pounds for parking, cash only, immediate payment. All proceeds to the Winter Warmer Fund."

"Thirty pounds? We're on a public road," the pap complained.

"Public road, private land, public nuisance," Meredith chimed in sweetly, pointing at the tin can she'd duct-taped to our garden wall with *PAY & DISPLAY* scrawled in gold marker. "No pay, no stay."

Shannon swept in, cheerfully lethal. "Tickets for the Christmas Cèilidh are also available," she trilled, holding a book of hand-made tickets like a Vegas dealer. "Usually they're thirty quid each, but for you lads, we'll do twenty. Comes with a free candy cane and a stern lecture about tres-passing."

I smirked. The Christmas Cèilidh was two quid a ticket.

"Ladies," a man from the third car said, trying a smile he probably saved for door staff, "we don't want trouble."

"Perfect," Esther said. "Neither do we. That'll be thirty

quid for parking, four tickets to the ball, and a fiver for the sausage rolls you've been eyeing since you got out of your car."

Cherise spread out her hands to indicate the basket of rolls from the bakery she had at her side.

"I don't want a sausage roll."

"You do," Meredith said, already bagging them up with the force of destiny. "It's for charity."

Gregory materialized from nowhere, wearing his "Honorary Bitch" badge and a glower that could sour milk. "And if any one of ye steps past that gate, I'll let these ladies show you what type of damage can be done with a knitting needle."

"We're not here for trouble," Parka repeated, gaze sliding toward the upstairs windows. "We just need a shot of Mr. Byrne. Then we'll be out of your hair."

"Then you're in the wrong place," Esther said. "We've only got a John Smith."

"I love them," I said, pleased with their ferocity. Kingsbarns always stood for their own.

Behind me, the front bell dinged with the energy of doom. My guests had come downstairs.

I pasted on a smile and closed the door behind me, stepping into the foyer, where our Italian couple huddled with their luggage and the American clutched a newspaper to her chest like a shield.

"Skye," the American said gravely, as if delivering news about a beloved but disreputable relative, "your front garden has turned into the BBC."

"They're not from the BBC," I scoffed. "They're ... freelancers."

The Italian woman wrinkled her nose adorably. "We cannot stay. We adore your inn, but the paparazzi outside the window, they make the romance … eh …"—she rotated her wrists helplessly—"limp."

"Flat," her husband supplied.

"Flat," she agreed. "We will go to St. Andrews where there is more peace."

"I completely understand," I said, my smile starting to hurt my face. "I'll comp your last night and help you book a taxi."

"They're blocking the lane," the American observed helpfully out the window.

"I'll get Gregory to move them," I said, with the breezy confidence of a woman who would absolutely send Gregory out to menace the vans with pebbles.

The German pair came down at nine sharp with backpacks and expressions set to "efficient disappointment." By ten thirty, the inn was a hollowed-out shell. Biscuits uneaten, bookings canceled, my bank account looking at me like it needed a hot-water bottle and encouraging words. Outside, the Book Bitches rousingly caroled *O Come, All Ye Faithful* at a volume and a key likely chosen to specifically disrupt audio recording.

I retreated to the front desk with my ledger and my pride and a smile so brittle I was worried my jaw would lock. Noah appeared at my elbow, which I absolutely did not find comforting.

He looked unfairly good in a jumper and a baseball hat pulled low over his head.

"Hey." His voice lowered. "You okay?"

"I'm thrilled," I said brightly. "I've always wanted to conduct a stress test on my business."

He leaned on the desk like he'd forgotten he was public property. I glanced up, glad I'd pulled the curtains closed.

"I can help."

"With what, exactly? Waving at the cameras in a way that says 'move along'? Writing a new song called 'Get Off Skye's Drive'?"

He slanted a look at me. "I was thinking more like ... I could cook. Make sure the Book Bitches have enough tea so they don't decide to body-check someone into the kirk. And also ..."—he tapped the ledger with one finger—"... this."

My laugh was sharp as glass. "You want to help with my accounts?"

"I know numbers," he said, unoffended. "Tour budgets, overhead, that beautiful spreadsheet on how much bananas cost per show."

"Um, no offense, Noah, but we're literally in this position because of your lack of attention to numbers." I grimaced, but that was the truth of it.

Noah straightened, his face tightening.

"That's fair, but I worked with the numbers I was given. Which, apparently, were fake."

"I'm sorry." I sighed, and pushed the ledger away from me. "This isn't your problem to deal with."

"I know, Skye, I'm not trying to take over, I'm just trying to help."

"That is what people say right before they take over," I snapped, and winced at myself.

He studied me for a long beat. "Skye."

"What?"

"How long have you been holding this together with duct tape and stubbornness?"

"I don't know what you mean," I lied.

"Your boiler apologizes when it works. Your radiator sounds like an elderly pug. The wallpaper in the blue room has air bubbles. You're doing the work of three people and eating toast standing up over the sink."

"I ..." I didn't know what to say.

Noah looked back at me. "Let me help."

"I don't want you to see it," I blurted. When his brow furrowed, I huffed out the rest. "The messy bits. The places where it's threadbare. The places where *I'm* threadbare."

His face did a thing that had nothing to do with pity and everything to do with recognition. "Skye."

"Don't," I warned.

"I already see it," he said gently. "I'm not here to be impressed. I'm here because being with you is the only place that's every felt right to me."

That ridiculous, unhelpful ache in my chest yawned open. I slammed the ledger shut before any actual feelings could escape and changed the subject, because it was the only defense I possessed.

"Why do you care if I'm still songwriting?" I asked, surprising myself, but desperate for a change of subject.

"Because you should be doing it," he said simply, creases fanning out from the corner of his eyes as he studied me, trying to follow along with my erratic thoughts. "You always should have been. You were the best of us."

"I run an inn now, Noah," I said, again, like repetition could make truth into excuse. "I do laundry. I change sheets. I unclog showers. I don't sit around waiting for a muse."

"You used to write in laundromats," he said. "On buses. In queues. Once on the back of my hand when you couldn't find a notebook."

"That was because you'd lost the notebook," I said, stabbing a pencil into the jar.

"You married a man who didn't mind that you worked yourself into the ground," he said, too carefully neutral to be casual. "Why?"

"Do we have to—"

"Yes."

I stared across my small lobby until the room blurred. "He was ... nice," I said finally. "Safe. He thought love meant never raising your voice. He liked spreadsheets and new tires and the same toast every morning."

"And you left," Noah said, not a question.

"I left," I said. "Because 'safe' started feeling like 'silent.' Because I forgot what my own voice sounded like unless I was telling someone about check-out time. Because he made me feel like a set of good habits and not a person. Because he wanted kids and I ..." I cleared my throat. "I didn't."

"That's perfectly fine to not want that, Skye. I never did either," Noah reminded me. I'd forgotten that about him. "Though I'll admit ... a part of me broke when I heard you'd married."

"I read the magazines at the hairdresser," I said dryly, raising an eyebrow at him. "You dated many a famous woman, Noah. Was it an oil heiress? Or that producer who made a record that sounded like a migraine?"

"I loved two of them," he said, and the honesty made me blink. "Not ... well. Not in a grown way. I loved being loved. I loved not being alone on the road."

"Honest," I said, impressed and yet, so very irritated.

"I hate that I didn't fight harder for us," he said, the words dropping into the room like coins into a poor box. "I should have, Skye. You were worth it."

The room stilled. The house shifted around me, the room closing in, as my thoughts scrambled. This was a hell of a conversation to be having on a random Tuesday morning.

But isn't that when all life-changing conversations happen? When you least expect them?

From outside, Esther's voice rose on the wind. "Parking rates have just switched to hourly. Ten pounds for an hour and a compliment for Cherise's hat or I'll read you my thoughts on Dickens."

My phone dinged and I glanced down to see a cancellation notification, and an email from another.

"The rest of my guests coming this week just canceled," I murmured, deflating. "Look at that."

"So it's just us."

"Just us," I repeated, the words working their way through me and igniting my core with need.

Along with anxiety. *I have no income now for the foreseeable future. Bloody hell.* How was that going to work? Would I have to close the inn? The last thing I wanted was to fail Gran.

Voices rose outside, and I stood and crossed the room to peek out the door. More cars had arrived, and Harper and Rosie had joined the Book Bitches in their standoff.

They'd brought chairs, and someone had dragged a small fire pit onto my lawn. Gregory was squatting and building the base for a fire, while Cherise was flirting with a man whose cheeks had gone pink at the attention.

"I brought my guitar," Noah offered. "Maybe you've got a few half-finished songs sitting around. Want to give it a go?"

It felt like he was asking so much more.

We stood on either side of the room. The inn breathed. The wind rattled the old glass. Outside, the Book Bitches started *Jingle Bells* in a key previously unknown to science. And even though it was just confirmed that the inn would probably have to close, Noah wanted to make music. Did he really not care that I was losing my gran's business?

I pushed past him to the hallway because I couldn't be in a room with him right now. My emotions were pinging around inside, like too many balls loose in a pinball machine, and I wasn't sure I could trust what I said next. I paused when I realized he was following me and turned. While a part of me did want to make music with him again—desperately—I was also worried about my inn.

For some reason, we looked up at the same time.

"Mm," Noah said, a surprised look on his face. "That wasn't there before."

Mistletoe.

Hanging right in the center of the arch, its pearly berries looking smug, leaves tied in a green satin bow made from Gran's ribbons.

"I didn't put that there," I rushed out.

"Esther?" he guessed, craning his neck.

"Esther would have posted a sign," I said faintly. "With rules."

"Rosie?"

"She'd have strung fairy lights around it and a footnote about informed consent."

He looked at me. "Gran?"

"Stress," I said immediately, too loudly. "This is stress. We do *not* have a ghost."

We didn't move. *Of course* we didn't move. The hallway seemed to pull in on itself, the old plaster holding its breath, the wind outside lifting its chin to see better. The Book Bitches launched into *Silent Night* like an unlicensed Greek chorus. Somewhere, a car door slammed.

He stepped in and I felt the heat of him like a hand at my back. It had always been like that. He was so tall, so strong, and whenever I was near him, he seemed to be able to envelop me. *I've longed to be this close to this man again. I missed his touch.* I'd never admitted that out loud, but the heat between us—*the love*—had been insanely amazing. And here we were, together, the mistletoe hung above us, a question unanswered.

"House rules?" he asked.

"No songs about me," I said, because if I stopped being ridiculous, I'd start being honest, and we could not have that on a weekday. "No paparazzi. No touching"—my mouth betrayed me—"without asking."

He swallowed. "Skye."

"Noah."

"Can I—" He stopped, closed his eyes, opened them. "Can we forget about the past for a moment? I'm dying to taste you again."

"Yes," I said, a tremble working through me. "We can do that."

His lips slid over mine, both a promise and a memory, and my heart shivered. Tilting my head, he licked softly into my mouth, his tongue sliding against mine, and heat ignited in my core. We'd always been this way. Our chemistry was palpable, and I moaned into his mouth and threaded my arms around his neck.

He lingered, savoring my kiss, never rushing. Desire threaded through me, a longing so sharp it hurt, and I arched against him, loving the slide of his tongue across mine, the way his teeth scraped lightly against my lower lip. He bumped me lightly back against the doorframe, his hands stroking down my back, cupping my bum and pulling me closer to him. I gasped against the friction of him, the longing building inside me, and sank further into the kiss.

"God, Skye. I've missed you," Noah said while breaking away. Our eyes met, so many words unsung, and then he took me under again. He slid his hands beneath my jumper, finding my skin, and I shivered at his touch. Lovely liquid heat slipped through me, and I rocked lightly against his hard body. His lips were demanding, coaxing me to give every inch of myself over to the kiss, and when we finally broke apart, my chest was heaving, and my body was flushed with need.

Bloody hell, but I wanted to grab his hand and pull him upstairs. I wanted to feel the weight of his body against mine, leaning over me and filling me so that I didn't have to think about yesterdays or tomorrows. He made me want to feel again.

"Whoever put that up," he said, his voice decidedly cheerful, "has a dark sense of humor."

"I'm burning it after dinner," I said, already knowing I wouldn't.

"Liar," he said, his mouth quirking up in that shit-eating grin he had.

"Obviously," I sighed. My lips still burned from his kiss. Of course, I was going to keep the mistletoe up. Now that I had the taste of his kiss on my lips again, I wasn't sure I'd ever stop craving it.

Outside, Esther's voice rose. "That's four tickets and two slices of Dundee cake! Now sing, you vultures!" The paparazzi, to their credit, tried to harmonize. I snorted.

"Those poor bastards have no idea what they're dealing with." Noah laughed.

The phone on the front desk rang, and I glanced at it, the moment broken.

"Go on," Noah said, running a finger across my cheek. "I know you have business to deal with. I'll make myself useful by bleeding all the radiators now that the rooms are empty."

I went to answer a call that I knew would be another cancellation, and he went to find the radiator key. The mistletoe stayed where it was, smug as a cat, and the inn watched us with the indulgence of old buildings who knew how the story went even when the people in it pretended they didn't.

Eight

NOAH

By midday the siege had developed a festive mood, which is the most Kingsbarns sentence I can think of.

Word spread faster than scandal here—across the green, down the lane, through the bakery where the sisters weaponized shortbread. People took shifts outside the inn like it was D-day and the enemy was polyester parkas. Esther set up a folding table and declared it *Headquarters*. Gregory became Head of Security, wearing a whistle and the expression of a man who has been waiting his whole life to use it. Cherise managed a thermos station. Shannon acquired a megaphone and should never be allowed to own one again. Meredith produced a plastic cash box from her handbag like a magician pulling out a rabbit and started selling everything that wasn't nailed down for the Winter Warmer Fund.

The paparazzi tried to be professional.

Whenever a lens angled toward the door, the Book Bitches would immediately burst into a carol at a volume that rendered audio useless and made the paps groan. When someone tried to wedge a foot through the gate, Gregory blew his whistle and fixed them with a stare that made their ancestors feel judged. The school kids arrived with hand-lettered signs: *ESTHER FOR PRIME MINISTER* and *BUY A RAFFLE TICKET OR GO HOME.* Rosie and Harper delivered mulled cider and a stack of photocopied "Know Your Rights" sheets for villagers dealing with "overly enthusiastic media professionals."

"We've invented a street faire," I told Skye, peeking through a small hole in the curtain.

"We've invented probable cause," she muttered, then leaned closer to the glass despite herself. "Is Shannon shaking them down for tickets for their extended families?"

"Ten quid for plus-ones." I'd listened. "Meredith's upselling the Dundee cake. Esther's insisting on exact change."

I still hadn't turned my phone on. I knew I'd have to face the world at some point, but I'd wait until the paps had their next story. There was always something else that would draw their attention.

Inside the inn, it got quiet.

Skye shooed me away from her books and I took to the lounge, sitting on the floor in case there were any gaps in the curtains, and stoking the fire as I scribbled lines to a song that had been bouncing around my head ever since I'd returned home.

After a while, Skye brought a bottle of wine and

uncorked it with the competence of a woman who has held a house together with faith and a laundered tea towel, then she poured it into two mismatched goblets.

"I thought, at this point, we might as well." Skye gave me a wry grin, and despite my worry over my career tanking in flames, I smiled back.

Because when everything was falling apart, what else could you do but drink wine on the floor with the love of your life?

We sat on the floor with our backs to the sofa and sipped our wine, watching the flames dance in the grate. The fire popped.

"Show me your songs," I said, not because I thought it was wise but because sometimes the shortest road to a thing is through.

She didn't move for a long breath. Then she put her goblet down, stood, and disappeared up the stairs, her footsteps growing softer the farther away she got from me.

I stared at the fire and thought about my past sins. What I'd gained. What I'd lost.

I'd been just a kid, really, barely twenty-two—a record contract on the line. Skye had refused to sign because of the manager we eventually signed with. *I* told her that she was a fool who didn't know any better. *I* told her that we could achieve what we'd always wanted. She'd wanted our success, I knew that, but not if it came with working with someone she didn't trust.

So she'd left.

And broken my heart.

And I'd broken hers.

It was all muddled now, softened around the edges, with the way time does to memories.

Skye came back with a shoebox, and my breath caught as she walked in the room, eyes huge in her face. She was still the most beautiful woman I'd ever seen.

It had always been her. The one who made my heart sing.

Skye sat cross-legged on the rug, set the box between us like a living thing, and took off the lid.

Notebooks. Receipts. The backs of flyers. A napkin from a café in St. Andrews with a ring of tea on it, and in the circle, five words I could tell were hers … *teach my mouth mercy first.*

"I know it looks like a mess," Skye said, looking up at me, the reflection of the flames glinting in her eyes.

"It looks like a life," I said.

She sifted the stack as if she were divining the right scrap the way you find shells on the beach. She pulled a folded sheet from an old spiral notebook and stared at it long enough for me to realize I was holding my breath.

"It's not a song," she said.

"What is it?"

"A chorus that kept pretending to be one." She cleared her throat, eyes on the page. "It's not … great."

"Most things aren't when they're honest," I said.

Her mouth twitched. She handed it over.

The handwriting was round, urgent, a tiny leftward slant like she was leaning into wind. The words weren't pretty. They didn't try to be.

If I come back, let it be softer,
corners sanded by the years.

Let the floorboards learn our footfall,
let the heart forget our tears.
If I come back, let it be braver,
no white flags at the door.
If I come back, let it be choosing,
not running like before.

"Not a song," she repeated. "Just … a begging letter, I guess."

My throat tightened. I handed it back like I was returning a relic.

"Verse?" I asked, instead of the ten things I wanted to say.

"I don't have one," she said. "I have these." She brandished a handful of scraps of paper. "They don't go together."

"That's half the job, as you know," I said. "What do they want?"

"To be taken seriously." She laughed softly. "They want to stop being in a shoebox."

Outside, the Book Bitches had gotten into an argument about whether angels have wings or were more high-tech these days and rode segways.

I pulled my guitar case toward me and opened it without ceremony. The guitar wasn't my touring one. It was just my old favorite. My constant. I tuned by muscle memory while Skye paged through scraps she pretended not to be attached to.

"Let's start from the middle," I said, when Skye made a frustrated noise. "Write the chorus like it's a promise you're scared to make."

"I'm not writing a song about me," she said quickly.

"It's not about you," I said. "It's about someone who sounds like you. Anyone who has ever felt like you." I played a chord.

She made a face, but the kind you make when someone's handed you a biscuit and you said you weren't hungry. "Four chords?" she asked, resigned and fond. "You still a four-chord man?"

"When I'm trying to be honest." I strummed a chord and built on it. I played it once, twice, let it settle. Her shoulders dropped a half inch.

"Give me the first line," I said. "Not the best line. The first one."

She sifted. Squinted. Chose. "I'm not the girl who held your chorus while the kettle learned to sing."

"That'll do," I said softly, and my fingers found the chord without asking me. "Okay. Keep going."

She shook her head, panicked and amused. "Don't look at me."

"I'm looking at the fire," I lied. It was impossible not to look at Skye when she wrote songs. Her face lit from within, her eyes going soft and dreamy and somewhere else, and I wanted to follow her there, wherever her dreams took her.

We fought our way to a verse the way you fight through the brush to get to the water. Cursing and laughing when we got snagged. I threw words at her and she threw better ones back. We let the lines come when they wanted. We didn't force it. I tried a melody. She shook her head. I tried another and she nodded.

Outside, the light fell out of the sky and left us with the reflected glow of a village deciding to be louder than money.

Someone brought fairy lights. Someone else had brought speakers and Esther was now standing at a table, headphones half on, pretending she was DJing a set at Glastonbury.

We stayed on the floor like heathens and built something fragile and stubborn.

It wasn't polished. It didn't need to be. It sounded like us fifteen years ago if we'd learned to apologize in the middle of a fight.

We opened another bottle of wine and ate the scones she'd baked for her now-departed guests.

Skye's voice found the melody like it had been waiting to come home, but not showy. She sang like she was politely asking the words to endure her. When she forgot herself, her hand lifted out of habit, fingers cueing air. I matched it without thinking.

"Bridge," I said, because we were doing this.

"I don't have anything left," she said on a half laugh. "There's nothing left in the box."

"Then write something you don't have," I said. "Write a line like a dare."

She bit her lip and the moment stretched between us.

She spoke first. "If we come back, come back hungry, don't feed us ghosts or bread made of lies."

There she was. There was my girl.

We looked at each other and grinned. For a second we were twenty-two and freezing and sure of only this, that music was the one honest magic and we were lucky to have a trick that worked.

"Again," she said, not smiling, and we sang a bridge that would take the weight if it had to.

We ran the whole thing once, twice. It wasn't ready to show anyone. It might never be. That wasn't the point. The point was there was something new between us that wasn't a wound.

"You were right," she said finally, voice small. "I put them in a shoebox so they couldn't hurt me."

"I've been singing mine at stadiums so they look big enough to be afraid of," I said. "Neither strategy seems to have worked spectacularly."

She made a tired, incredulous sound that was almost a laugh. "My divorce lawyer would agree with you."

"You don't have to—"

"It wasn't a tragedy," she said, looking at the fire. "It was two decent people who didn't bring enough to the table. We were good at talking about mortgages and bad at talking about fear. We tried. We failed kindly. He's married to a teacher now. They have a baby on the way and a dog named Button. I think he's happy."

"And you?" I asked, already knowing I was greedy for her answer.

"I'm learning how to be a person again," she said. "Not a cautionary tale. Just ... Skye. She's mouthier than I remembered."

"I like her," I said, hoping my voice didn't betray the bit of me that wanted to kneel on the rug and make promises I didn't yet know if I could keep.

She turned her head, her cheek pressed into her knee. "And you? Do you love anything besides an adoring crowd?"

"I love the moment before the first chord when the room decides to love you just for being you," I admitted, leaning back. "I loved two women badly and left them when they asked for the bit I keep in a locked drawer. I don't want to be that boy again. The one who chooses fame over his heart."

"Then don't," she said.

The space between us narrowed.

I slid forward on the rug until my knees touched hers. My nerves were shot. This felt worse and better than stepping on any stage.

"Skye," I said, and my voice cracked on the *K* because I was desperate to touch her again.

"Noah," she returned.

"Can I—" I refused to be the man who didn't ask.

"Yes," she said, and saved my life.

Rolling onto my back, I pulled her with me, so she lay stretched over me, body to body, her lips on mine. I arched against her as need took over, wanting my hands on that beautiful body of hers.

"Noah." Skye pulled back as I tugged at the hem of her shirt, needing it off. "I'm not the young girl I once was."

"Thank God for that," I murmured, drawing the shirt over her head as she sat up and straddled me. She was both softer and stronger than she'd been then, and I exulted in every inch of delicious skin that was revealed. Aye, she was softer in some areas, but soft was fun to touch. I stroked my fingers up her side and brushed my knuckle across the bottom of her breast.

Skye sucked in a breath and bit her teeth into her bottom lip, and I grinned up at her. I'd seen her make that same expression many times before and I moaned as she rocked her hips against me, torturing me.

The light haloed her hair, making it look on fire around her head, and her face was loose and relaxed as I leaned up to unclip her bra. Catching her mouth with mine, I nibbled at her lower lip as I slid the strap down her arm, following its path with my lips. Skye giggled as I nipped at the inside of her wrist, and then turning, scraped my teeth lightly over her nipple. Groaning, she threw her head back, offering her breasts to me like a dessert, and I dove in, eager to taste them once again.

Skye mewled softly as I cupped both breasts with my hands, rubbing my thumbs across hard nipples, and then licked wetly across the pebbled skin of each pointed tip. Blowing a hot breath, I sunk my teeth in, just a touch harder—just the way I knew she liked it.

Skye bit back a louder moan, and I brought my head up, swallowing the sound with a kiss. My tongue slid against hers, wet and hot, and I groaned as she rocked against me, her need clear.

"Tell me you have a condom."

"Always," I said. Easing her to the side, I slid my trousers off and pulled out my wallet and Skye hiccupped out a laugh.

"What?" I looked up at her.

"Just you sitting here on the floor with your shirt on, no pants, and a condom in your wallet." She shook her head at me. "Some things never do change, do they?"

"And some things do." I pulled her over me, my need for her now desperate. Did she have any clue how I felt about her? Skye had been my wildfire, my warmth, and a part of me had gone cold the day she'd walked away.

Sliding inside her again ignited me.

I wanted to touch and taste every last bit of her. I gasped as she reared back, bracing herself on her hands, and began to ride me, her hips moving as urgently as my hands did across her body. Reaching out to the V of her legs, I slid my fingers over her, finding how wet she was around me, and rubbed.

Skye's breath caught, and her pace quickened, and I dropped back, watching this glorious goddess, her amber hair tumbling down her shoulders, take her bliss against me.

Pleasure rose, a wave inside me, as I thrust into her, hard against her soft, loving the feel of her as she rocked against me. Her muscles tightened, drawing me deep, and my desire skyrocketed. She picked up the pace, and I met her, thrusting hard from beneath her, matching her, beat for beat, until we finished the song our bodies were making together.

It was one of the best moments of my life and when we both broke at the same time, shuddering in ecstasy and relief, a part of me died.

And I was pretty sure I didn't want that part back.

Because how? How would I ever be able to let her go again?

Outside, Esther's laugh rang like a bell as she cued up a new DJ set and music blared. The twinkle lights bounced across the ceiling, and I, who had made a living out of pretending, sat on a rug and believed in something as stupid and frightening as hope.

Nine

SKYE

The news broke by mid-afternoon the next day.

Noah Byrne cleared of wrongdoing.

A presenter with swishy blond hair called Noah "an unwitting victim of a trusted adviser" in that polished, sympathetic tone they save for rescued seals and handsome men with tragic eyes.

I put my phone face down on the counter and stared at the toaster.

By the time I'd finished making tea, I'd received a dozen texts.

Don't let his ego get too inflated, or he'll be unbearable.

· · ·

Noah padded into the kitchen in socks, hair still sleep-ruffled, and read the text message over my shoulder.

"Och, I'm the unbearable one?" Noah asked. "You saw what happened when you gave Esther a microphone."

Turning, I slid into his arms and chuckled.

"True. She's an absolute menace."

"Apparently I didn't help embezzle millions," he said.

"Congratulations on officially not being a criminal."

He hugged me tighter, and I burrowed my face into his chest.

"God, Skye. You were right. About it all. I hate what trusting him meant for us."

It was tough to hear the regret in his voice. *All those years lost.*

Shaking it off, because there was no use trying to change the past, I left his arms and put the kettle on, because that's what we did when emotions got the best of us.

It was all too new, and at the same time, so very old ... for me to really unravel all the complicated feelings that the night before had brought for me. Being with Noah again had been amazing, our chemistry had always been off the charts, but I wondered if that was the easy part. Giving ourselves to each other was as natural as taking my next breath, but now in the bright light of morning, I worried that my heart just might not be able to handle watching him walk away again.

Outside, the siege had turned into a carnival. Word got out that tonight's Christmas concert would go on—as if Esther would ever let a little fraud and international scandal ruin her event—and the village hall sold tickets faster than mince pies at the bakery. There was no hiding the fact that Noah would be playing at the concert, nor did I think they tried. Now that he'd been exonerated, it was time for him to sing for his supper, so to speak. Kingsbarns had stood for him, now it was time for him to repay the favor. The paparazzi, having been strong-armed into paying for parking and forced to sing carols off-key as penance, bought tickets too, even though they'd been warned about filming during the event.

By half four, Noah had been smuggled into the hall by way of laundry bags being taken to the laundromat. Esther coordinated his movements like she was a spy in the military, with detailed instructions. I was surprised she hadn't gotten herself a walkie-talkie.

"Let them have their fun," Noah said, pulling a laundry bag over his head in the back of my car.

"You have to be careful how much leave you give them," I warned him, but he only chuckled as I slammed the door and drove the long way to the village community center.

The center was one of those multi-purpose places with a large open room and a stage that has seen everything from nativity plays to furious debates about bin collection. Tartan bunting swooped from beam to beam, a forest of poinsettias lined the front, and someone had fashioned a photo backdrop with paper stars and the words *A Very Kingsbarns Christmas* in letters cut from glitter card.

In the back room, the kids' choir buzzed like a shaken bottle of Irn-Bru. Cherise organized folding chairs while Shannon poured wine into paper cups. Esther, clipboard under her arm, wore a silver headband that said "Director" in rhinestones and the aura of a woman who was ready to yell at you if you stepped out of line.

"You're late but also early," she pronounced, which is peak Esther. "We're running ten minutes behind and two steps ahead."

"What does that even mean?" I asked, but she was already turning to bark at a teenager who'd wandered off with the microphone.

The Book Bitches were rehearsing their skit—because of course they were. Tonight's pièce de résistance was a short reenactment of *Pride & Prejudice*.

Apparently, they'd looped Esther's husband in to play Mr. Darcy, and Wallace, the pub's warrior kitten, was set to make his stage debut.

Harper slid up beside me, handing me a paper cup of wine and a conspiratorial grin. "How's your stomach?"

"Anxious," I said.

"Good," she said. "Means you're about to do something that matters. Also, look." She nodded toward the side door. Two men with expensive cameras waited in the corridor, shivering in their parkas, clutching tickets. "We made them buy programs."

"You made programs?" I laughed. "How much did you charge?"

"Whatever they had in their wallets, plus a promise to clap for the pensioners."

Rosie popped up like a ribbon. "Also, we've reserved the first two rows for the kids and their parents. The paps are at the back where the cheap seats are."

My stomach swooped, and I tried to ignore it. This

would be fine. Noah was used to performing for much larger crowds.

I found Noah by the stage door, tuning his guitar. He looked different. Lighter, somehow. The jumpy, hunted light had gone from behind his eyes. They also warmed when they saw me and I tried ignoring the shiver of excitement that danced through me at his look.

"You're on after the nativity chaos," I said.

"Good," he said, plucking a string. "They'll be the headliners. I'm the warm-down act."

"You're ridiculous," I said. "You also don't have to do this, you know. The paps are still here."

"I said I would do it, so I am," he said, his eyes creasing at the corner as he smiled. "Think I can get a glitter banner that says *Innocent* hung over the stage?"

"Esther will hang you if you touch her set."

"Fair," he said, and his smile slid sideways into something softer. "Skye."

"What?"

"I want to sing what we wrote. Last night."

My mouth went dry. "Noah—"

"With you," he said quickly. "Only ... only if you want to. No names. Our way. But I ... want to stand in front of them"—he tipped his head toward the murmur of the hall —"and sing something we built together."

The shoebox flashed in my head. The scraps. The bridge we'd hammered into place like two people repairing a fence in the rain. Fear whirled in me. And then something else ... a thread of joy that felt like a high wire, dangerous and exactly my kind of view.

"House rules," I said, my last defense. "No songs about me."

"It isn't," he said, steady. His stormy eyes held mine. "It's about choosing to come back through the front door."

"Fine," I said, and my heart hammered in my chest. "But you'd better catch me if I fall."

"You won't." Noah looked away and then back up at me. "I'll never let you down again, Skye."

I didn't know what to do with that, even though my heart felt like filled to bursting at his words. Could I trust him again? Noah wasn't a stupid young man anymore, but he also was mega famous. A part of me worried that once again, our timing wasn't right.

Had I been stupid to even let him into my home? My arms? My bed?

Nerves hammered me as I went to take a seat to watch the Book Bitches' riotous performance.

Esther burst onstage with the excitement of a woman who put something stronger than sugar in her coffee every morning. "Welcome, welcome!" she boomed. "Thank you for braving the elements, the economy, and our parking stewards. Tonight, we celebrate community, kindness, and of course, love. Please turn off your phones and remember this is a family show. Swearing will be done by me backstage only."

Laughter warmed the room. The program rolled on. The kids' choir looked adorable in tea towels and wings that shed glitter like dandruff, warbling through *Away in a Manger* with alarming sincerity, the pensioners' handbell ensemble ringing *Carol of the Bells* as if they'd discovered heavy metal,

Gregory and Cherise performing a duet that consisted entirely of him glowering while she sang like a contented robin. The paps sat at the back with their lenses, surprisingly well-behaved, probably because every time they so much as shifted their weight, a dozen villagers swiveled in unison and glared.

I laughed as Meredith swept out as Mrs. Bennet with pearls, a floral housecoat, and a hand fan. "Girls! The Kingsbarns Inn is let. And to a single man of *fortune* who will *donate* to the Winter Warmer Fund!"

I laughed as they mentioned my inn. I had hope that guests would return in the new year now.

Esther's husband, Daniel, in a tragic cravat, arrived as Mr. Darcy.

"I have standards," he intoned and brought the house down. By the time Esther had arrived as Elizabeth and the cat, Wallace, apparently was standing in for Mr. Bennet, the entire hall was in tears of laughter.

A confetti cannon fired. Esther took the shower of sparkles like a coronation.

"Intermission," she cried, wiping glitter from her eyelashes and likely calculating the till in her head. "Fifteen minutes. Buy biscuits or be declared a scrooge."

During the break, half the village drifted toward the back to harass the press while I slipped to the back room to check on Noah.

Everyone in the room was pretending not to look at him as he lightly strummed his guitar, focusing on the paper in front of him, and I was struck by how many times I'd seen that silhouette in the press. Noah had lived a million lives since he'd left me. Even if Glen had screwed him over, maybe it had been worth it? Maybe I'd been in the wrong to leave.

"All good?" I asked, suddenly feeling awkward around him.

"Aye, lass. Now that you're here." He smiled up at me and the Book Bitches let out a collective sigh of adoration behind me.

He stood and walked to the door, nodding at people as he went, and then stepped onto the stage. I followed, leaning in the doorframe just off the side of the stage where people couldn't see me, and watched as he strode confidently to the microphone.

I could feel the shift in the room like a held breath.

Esther, to her credit, did not announce Noah. He didn't need it. She simply said, "All right then," and vanished into the wings.

"Evening," he said, voice steady and warm. "Thanks for keeping our village kinder than the world, and for making the men with cameras buy baked goods."

Laughter rose, warm and sharp.

"I'm going to sing two songs you know," he said, "and one you don't. The one you don't was written around a fireplace with a good bottle of wine and an honest look at the past."

He played a holiday song that belonged to everybody. Voices joined him without being asked. He let the hall sing itself, which is why I loved him then and now.

My heart skipped a beat.

Bloody hell, but I did love the man.

A part of me always had.

Always would.

He was impossible not to. His voice rising up, circling around me, dragging me under with his words.

He played a Christmas song the kids knew and he let them lead, all of us laughing and clapping along.

Then he looked toward the wings where I was standing with my hands clenched in front of me.

"I said I'd sing something new," he said. "But I'm not going to sing it alone."

The crowd turned as one to the wings. I swear the entire back row—press included—leaned forward, the way deer do when they hear a twig crack. Rosie tipped her chin at me and Harper squeezed my hand. Esther shoved me hard enough to send me two steps forward, and I glared at her over my shoulder.

"*Go,*" Esther mouthed.

I walked out.

The cameras at the back rose like a glittering tide, even though the locals turned to growl at them. I saw their lenses, their black glass, the awful hungry attention of them and for a second, my legs wanted to turn and bolt straight through the cardboard stable and into the cold. Then I found Noah's eyes. The years fell away. He looked exactly like a boy in a freezing garage offering me a chord.

He held out the second mic.

I took it with trembling hands.

He started the progression we'd built on the rug. Soft, with room around it. I heard the first line in my head like a dare and then I said it out loud, into a microphone, in front of the village and the press and the universe and my gran.

"I'm not the girl who held your chorus while the kettle learned to sing."

A ripple went through the room—not surprise, not shock—but recognition. Noah picked up the next line like a kindly echo.

"We're not the kids who ran for corners when we felt the edges sting."

I sang again and my voice didn't break. He sang under me and our harmony fit without ceremony. The bridge came like a door we'd left ajar and we walked through together. A little girl in the front row put her chin on the stage and just watched. The press leaned forward, their lenses humming.

I didn't die.

I didn't even wobble. My hand shook once, but Noah kept the tempo steady like a promise. Our words were simple and so was the melody, which is why it hurt less than it might have and more than I expected.

Then the room did that astonishing thing where it stayed quiet a heartbeat longer than necessary. There's a special kind of silence that colors in around you. And then, like someone let breath back into the world, it cracked and applause spilled up from the front row, bursting in the middle like confetti.

Noah reached for my free hand and I put my hand in his. Heat zinged up my arm and broke softly inside me, and then we lifted our clasped hands to cheers. The cameras caught it and I made the choice I hadn't made fifteen years ago.

I didn't let go.

We stood there in a worn village hall with tartan bunting and cardboard hay and a sign that said "No Flash Photography" while flashbulbs popped like fireworks.

Noah bowed a little. I bobbed, awkward, and laughed at myself.

In the back room, I slumped against the wall, my breath coming out in soft little pants. Noah leaned beside me, our shoulders brushing.

"Okay," I whispered. "Okay."

He turned his head. "Okay," he said back, the word full of everything left unsaid. The noise from the hall swelled again—Esther was announcing the raffle winners—and the world returned to ordinary magnitude.

But it wasn't ordinary.

I looked at Noah and didn't look away.

This time, if my name was caught in a song, it was because I'd put it there. And if the cameras took me with it, they could take me standing up.

Ten

NOAH

The pub was already loud when we walked in, but not the bad kind. The good kind—glasses clinking, a rumble of conversations, and somebody laughing too hard in the corner. The fire was going, the tree lights were on, and Harper and Reed were manning the bar.

"They're here," Shannon sang from her table, holding up her phone. "Have you seen?"

"Seen what?" Skye stiffened next to me, and I tugged her into the warm pub, the crowd parting for us like we were a hot knife slicing through butter.

"Let them in first," Esther said, shouldering through with a tray of sausage rolls and meat pies. "Phones down until you've eaten. That's a rule."

"Since when?" Meredith asked, already breaking it. "Oh my God. Look at this."

Everyone looked as Meredith held up her phone.

On Meredith's screen, a video played of the song Skye and I sang at the hall.

"It already has five hundred thousand views," Meredith said, turning the phone back to her, her voice hushed in awe. "Skye and Noah reunite. Is there a reunion tour around the corner?"

"Absolutely not." Skye laughed, but the stubborn lift of her chin set off warning bells in my gut.

Rosie, in a bright red sweater and a purple corduroy skirt, looked up from her phone. "You're trending," she said, sounding both delighted and deeply apologetic. "And before you ask, I did not post it. I don't have a death wish. The mums' WhatsApp group did. And then TikTok ate it."

"What's TikTok?" Gregory asked.

"A lifestyle," Rosie said. "And a trap."

Rosie scrolled the comments. People were being *nice*. I had not seen that on the internet in a long time. Things like *... the harmonies?!* and *who is she* and *I didn't know I needed this, but I did* and *come to my wedding and sing this, please, please, please.* A blog had already posted a clip calling it "a quiet sledgehammer."

"Look at this one," Rosie said, breathless. "'The song feels like when you get home and your love has a cup of tea waiting for you already.'"

"That's ... nice," Skye said, accepting the glass of wine Esther gave her and gulping half of it. Her hand shook.

Esther clapped her hands. "Phones down," she said. She didn't shout, but everyone heard her anyway. "First, we clap for Wallace. He was *magnificent*, wasn't he?"

Wallace prowled across the bar, still sporting a snazzy

tartan bow tie. He accepted a small avalanche of applause with a slow blink and a rude yawn. Meredith, who had sewn his little waistcoat out of an old velvet skirt, wiped her eyes with a napkin.

"Second," Esther continued, "we clap for Skye. Noah's used to performing, but it was Skye who brought that song home."

Skye's cheeks flushed a bright red, and I clapped the loudest of all. She had been magnificent, and singing with her felt like coming home.

My phone kept buzzing in my pocket, and I noticed several texts from my agent. Ignoring them, because I just wanted to live in the moment, I switched the phone off and accepted a wee dram of whisky from Daniel, who winked at me.

"I know this might be unwanted advice from a newly-wed," Daniel began and I grinned. He was in his late seventies and had married Esther in a whirlwind courtship just months prior. "But it's rare for love to come around twice. I'd think long and hard about what you're walking away from when you leave." He said it as if me leaving was an already understood fact. And he wasn't wrong. The plan had never been to stay.

I'd just needed a moment of respite.

A calm from the storm.

But my band needed me.

I had responsibilities.

A record contract.

Actually, that might be in the bin with the news about the record company. Which meant, for the first time in years, I might actually *not* be beholden to anyone.

But myself.

That was a new and interesting thought. Turning it over in my head, I watched as everyone gushed over Skye, and how she fumbled with accepting praise.

"Look at this comment." Rosie held up her phone. "She sings like she's telling a story to friends in her kitchen."

Skye's eyes softened. "I like that."

I did too. I liked everything about Skye. The girl she'd been and the woman she'd grown into.

Esther banged a spoon on the edge of a pint glass. "Toast!" she yelled. "Quiet, you lot."

The room settled.

Skye stood, smiling over at me.

"This will be quick," she said. "Because Esther is terrifying."

"I am," Esther confirmed.

"I know how to tame her," Daniel whispered in my ear, and bloody hell, but the man made my cheeks warm. That was not an image I needed in my head.

Skye looked around the room. "Thank you," she said. "For buying tickets when you didn't have to. For blocking the lane. For singing too loud on purpose. For letting me be me tonight." She swallowed. "And to Noah, for sharing his gift."

I stepped forward.

"It's you who shared your gift, Skye. You've always been the best of us."

The room took a collective sigh and then all said, "Awwww."

We all laughed and then Skye lifted her glass.

"To the Book Bitches," she said.

"To the Book Bitches," everyone answered, raising whatever they had. Even Wallace got a tiny shot glass of cream.

Skye looked for me. Found me. Held my gaze.

"And to second chances," she said.

We drank. I kept my eyes on her over the rim of the glass. She flushed, then laughed, then turned back to Shannon who was telling her a story.

Music started up in the corner—a fiddle, a bodhrán, someone with a guitar that managed to be mostly in tune. A band that wasn't a band. A proper session made up of whoever brought an instrument and knew when to join. The floor cleared a little.

I didn't join. I leaned on the bar and let it roll over me. It felt like ... being allowed to stand still. I hadn't had a lot of that lately.

"Hungry?" Skye asked, coming over with a plate of sausage rolls.

"Starving," I said, and meant more than food.

We ate in companionable silence while Esther argued with Cherise about what jumper to wear on Christmas Day. Harper snapped a photo of Wallace wearing his bow tie and posted it with the caption: *Leading man energy.*

"Do you miss it?" Skye asked, eyes flicking to my guitar case by the door.

"Tonight? No." I didn't dodge the question. "I miss the bit where the music belongs to the room instead of the label. This feels like that. I've missed this without knowing what to call it."

"Home," she said, not romantic. Just stating facts.

"Yeah." I took a breath. "I thought the road was home. I

liked the moving. No one expects you to fix a boiler when you're in a hotel. No one calls at six a.m. about the bins."

"Bins are a big part of adulthood," she said, her mouth quirking up at the corners. "Nobody tells you that."

"The road stopped being fun when the rooms all looked the same," I said. "I kept trying to write my way out of it. Turns out I might have needed to sit still for a while."

"That's my business model," Skye said dryly. "So still moss can grow on me."

"Your business model works."

"Does it? Tell that to my guests. Oh wait, I still don't have any." Skye looked away.

I wished she would let me help, let me look at the books or make a list of needed repairs. But the stubborn lift of her chin told me everything I needed to know.

"Noah!" The chants went up and I finally put my hands in the air in defeat and went to join the band. We launched into a merry rendition of Amy Macdonald's *This is the Life*, and everyone clapped along.

An hour later, I was smiling so hard my face hurt.

I'd sold out stadiums, had tea with the late Queen, and traveled around the world.

But I couldn't quite remember the last time I'd had so much fun.

My soul had been craving this.

Impromptu and unhurried jam sessions with an audience that was more than willing to interrupt you if they didn't like what you played.

It was fun. It was easy. It was exactly what I'd needed.

Esther banged her hand on the table. "One more toast

and then I'm making Harper turn off the lights so you all go home," she said. "We're getting near closing."

Groans. Fake outrage. Everyone lifted their glasses anyway.

"To The Royal Unicorn," Esther said.

"To the Unicorn," the room answered.

She pointed a finger. "To John Smith."

"Boo," I said, smiling.

"No booing. He paid his parking," Meredith scolded.

"And to Skye," Esther said, "and the Kingsbarns Inn, which has brought so many fun and interesting people into our wee town for years now. We're blessed to have had you take up the helm when your gran passed, lass."

"To Skye," the room said, easy and true.

She went pink and laughed, thanking everyone. I let the sound land on me. I didn't know I needed that, but I did. Not the cheers. The belonging.

I picked up Skye's coat from the peg and held it out. She slid into it with a small sigh that got me right in the ribs.

"Walk?" I asked.

"Please," she said, which did a different thing to me. A good thing.

We spilled onto the street in a tumble of goodbyes and split off from the group. The night hit us clean and cold. Turning down the lane that led to the inn, the voices drifted away on the winter wind and our shoulders bumped companionably.

We didn't talk. We didn't need to. Our breath fogged the air, and somewhere a dog barked as their owner returned home. I put my hand out. Skye looked at it for a beat, like she was measuring something important. Then she took it.

My palm knew her. It sounded dramatic, like a lyric I would write, but it wasn't. It was simple. Warm. Right. We walked like that to the inn. No speech. No big declarations. Just ... us.

I used to think happiness came loud. Stadiums. Shouting. Hands in the air. Tonight it came quiet. Well, quiet-ish. A pub that smelled like woodsmoke and whisky. A village that knew your name and your business and looked after both. A woman who would tell you when you're being an idiot and feed you anyway. A cat in a bow tie. A song that felt like you built it with your hands.

At the inn, I opened the door and let her go in first. We stood in the foyer in the dim like teenagers who'd snuck in past curfew. The tree in the lounge threw balls of light across the ceiling.

Skye walked to the bottom of the stairs. Turning, she held out her hand, and warmth spread through me. Walking over, I took it, but before she could turn and pull me up the stairs, I bent my head and captured her lips in a searing kiss. I'd been aching to kiss her all night but hadn't been sure how she'd respond to public displays of affection. But for now? I didn't care what the future held.

I just wanted her.

I hadn't felt this calm in years. Not after a number-one hit. Not after a sold-out tour. Not after a single applause that went on so long it felt like it could carry me. This was different. This—Skye and me?—was all mine.

Eleven

SKYE

Laundry first. Always. When running a guesthouse, laundry was a constant. But it gave me ten minutes where I didn't have to think. Just fold. I stacked linens on the old pine table in the laundry room and made a neat wall out of cloth.

Noah was up before me this morning, having slipped out of bed early while whispering for me to stay. I knew he'd been avoiding answering his messages for a while, and you could only avoid life for so long.

Despite knowing that we'd gone viral the night before, I was surprisingly content. Last night had been ... big. The video. The pub. The feeling that the room was on our side. It sat in me like a warm brick.

Humming, I dumped a new load of towels into the

wash and then made my way toward the kitchen for my morning cup of tea.

Voices in the lounge stopped me.

Voices, plural. A male voice I didn't recognize—too bright. Salesman bright—then Noah's. Low. Careful.

I didn't mean to eavesdrop, but in the end, that's what I did.

I walked toward the sound and stopped just outside the doorway. Noah sat by the fire in a black jumper, hair a mess, one hand on the back of the sofa like he needed to grip the furniture to keep himself still. The other man wore a navy suit coat and a gold watch at his wrist. A sheaf of papers sat on the loveseat next to Noah.

"... is clean," the man said. "The press is sympathetic. We lock this down now and book you a showcase. London tonight, New York by the weekend. They want the story. New album. New chapter. Your duet is already clipping. This is the moment, Noah. This record deal is fantastic. It's a fresh start."

"I'm not going to London," Noah said. He sounded tired, not angry. "If we do it, we do it on terms that don't break me."

"Sure, sure," the man said fast, reassuring. "Creative control. Smaller rooms. But we need dates. We need a plan. And her." He flicked his eyes toward the stairs like he knew I was there. "They want *her*. You've seen the comments."

Noah turned and caught me hovering at the door. The air in the room shifted. The man half-turned, clocking me properly.

"Skye," Noah said. "This is Matt. My agent."

"Hi," I said, because manners are muscle memory. I

tucked a piece of hair behind my ear. My palms were damp. "Sorry to interrupt. Tea?"

"No time for tea," Matt said with a friendly smile. "We've got a flight in a few hours. I wanted to bring the paperwork so Noah could see there's a genuine offer. And to say congratulations, because last night was lightning in a bottle. We'd love to have you along with us."

"Thank you," I said. It came out flat, but that's how I felt.

Like a balloon with the air let out of it.

Matt looked between Noah and me and then cleared his throat. Standing, he smoothed his hands down his coat and looked down at Noah. "Ten minutes," he said. "I'll be outside."

And then Noah and I were alone with the contract and the fire and my stupid heart. Standing, Noah walked over to me.

"It's a good offer," he said, his voice soft.

My heart shifted inside me, pulling its walls up. I could see it in his face already. He was leaving. *He won't be staying for me.*

"It sounds like a significant offer," I said.

"It is." He nodded. "I told him I don't want a fast press run. I want time to write. I want to do it differently. But yes. It's big." Noah dug his hands in his pockets and rocked back on his heels.

"You should take it," I said. No hesitation, and that surprised even me. "You've worked for it. Your name is cleared. And, this is your career, Noah. You sang something good last night and people heard it. This is ... what you do."

"It doesn't have to be what I do without you." He

stepped closer and my breath hitched. "Come with me. Sing with me. Not as a plus-one. As you. Your voice is— Skye, your voice is the bit I've been looking for."

My chest gave a painful little twist. I looked down at the contract again so I didn't have to look at him. "I don't want to go on the road," I said, forcing the words out. "I like my mornings here. I like knowing which tap sticks and which guest will ask for extra towels. I like running out of coffee and having to sprint to the shop in my slippers. I like knowing where the spare fuses are."

"You can like all of that and still sing," he said, too fast, like he could outrun my no. "We could make this work. We could do long weekends. We could—"

"Noah," I said gently. "I'm not leaving my life to chase yours."

"It isn't chasing," he said, and now there was a thread of frustration lacing his voice. "It's building. Together. I have to think about my band, too. This isn't just about me."

"Which is why I think you should take it." I smiled though it didn't reach my heart.

"You're scared," Noah said. "You're scared to give your voice a chance. Your writing. It's easier to keep your dreams tucked away in a shoebox under your bed."

I felt it land. It wasn't cruel because he wasn't wrong, but it still pissed me off. "Don't call it fear because it doesn't match what you want."

"Skye."

"Yes, I'm scared," I said, before he could keep going. "I'm scared of getting swallowed whole. I'm scared of finding myself six months from now in some hotel corridor with my insides scraped out. I did the band thing. I watched who you had to become to survive it. I wasn't good at that then, and I won't be good at it now. But that isn't the same as hiding."

"You think I'm asking you to disappear into me," he said, running a frustrated hand through hair that I'd idly played with after we'd made love the night before. "I'm not."

"I think the machine is big," I said. "It's scary, Noah. Even if you do it smarter this time around. It's still a machine. I don't want to be a cog in it."

He rubbed a hand over his mouth. "I want you," he said, simply. "Not as a prop. As the person who made me remember why any of this matters. I want to write with you. I want to sing with you. I want to come back here and have this place be home. We can make it work."

"Last time we said we could make it work, too. We fought about a manager and blew up the band. I went home. You went bigger. We didn't talk for almost fifteen years. I'm choosing not to do that again." I shook my head.

"So that's it?" He wasn't angry. It was almost as if he couldn't really hear what I was saying.

"That's it," I said. My throat burned. I had to swallow before I could keep going. "Take the contract. Take the tour. Be good to yourself in the doing. Call me when you want to know whether the blue room radiator is leaking. Send me postcards. I'll cheer for you from here."

"And us?" he asked.

The word landed in the quiet that stretched between us. I clutched my hands so hard my nails dug into my palms.

"Timing isn't our friend," I said. "Maybe it never was.

I'm not asking you to choose me over this. I'm asking you not to ask me to leave my life. I can't do it, Noah."

He stepped back like he was just giving me space instead of falling away.

"Okay," he said, after an interminable beat. "I hear you."

"I'm sorry," I said, and I meant it.

"Don't be," he said, and there was the kindness I fell for when we were kids in a borrowed garage. "You told me the truth."

We stood there in silence that made you aware of your own heartbeat. He looked at me like he wanted to memorize something, and I looked at him like I was trying not to.

"I should pack," he said.

"Okay."

Noah crossed the room and paused in front of me. I lifted my chin and locked eyes with him, falling, as I always did, into the depths of his soul. Regret and something more flashed there.

"Skye ... I ..."

I waited and once again, for someone who had so many words to put into song, Noah couldn't seem to find any to say. Instead, he brushed his lips over my forehead in a kiss that made my eyes sting and left the lounge.

I stayed where I was until I heard his boots on the stairs and then I went into autopilot.

I put a fresh set of towels in the green room. I restocked the tea station. I went to the front desk, opened the ledger, and stared at a page I wasn't really reading.

Moments later, Noah came down the stairs with a bag and his guitar. He looked tired. Again.

I looked up when he set something on the table in front of me.

It was a guitar pick. Worn smooth at the edge. One of mine from years ago with a tiny star inked in the corner. I didn't remember drawing it, but I knew that I had.

"For when you want to finish something," he said. "Or start it."

"Thank you," I said, because I couldn't say anything else without crying.

Matt reappeared in the doorway. "Car's here," he said. He took in our faces. "We should go."

Noah looked at me, I looked back, but nobody moved.

"Come here," he said, and I rounded the desk. Pulling me into his arms, he kissed my forehead and I closed my eyes, breathing in the scent of him.

"I'll call," he promised.

"Don't if it makes it harder," I said. "Do if it doesn't."

Noah stepped back and picked up the guitar, then he stopped just at the door.

"Skye."

"Yes?" Silly, stupid, hope trembled in my heart.

"You were right about the boiler. It needs a new pump," he said, as if we could hide our goodbye inside a practical note.

"I know," I said, hope shattering. "I'll get it sorted." Somehow. Once my guests came back.

"Of course you will," he said, and then he was gone.

I returned to behind the desk and watched through the front window like a woman in a picture book. A fancy Land Rover with shiny rims was parked in front, and Matt rounded the bonnet while Noah put his guitar in the boot with care. He looked up once at the window. I stepped back so he couldn't see me and then stepped forward because I didn't want to hide. He lifted a hand. I lifted mine.

And then the car pulled away.

There's something so sad about watching a car pull away with someone you love in it. Not that I'd told Noah that I loved him, but my heart didn't know the difference.

The silence stretched out around me. The inn seemed to grow bigger, emptier, without his presence in it.

And then I shook my head and turned away because what else could I do?

The washer beeped its finished round and, numbly, I went to the laundry room and switched the loads. Then, sitting down in my empty inn, I made a list because that's what I did when I couldn't fix anything else.

"I'm okay," I said out loud, wondering if Gran could hear. It wasn't exactly a lie, but not also the whole truth either.

The bell over the front door dinged and I looked up, putting on my customer service smile.

Harper and Rosie stood there, the makings for mimosas in their hands, with the Book Bitches arguing at their backs.

"We saw him leave. This isn't the time to be alone," Harper said.

"We brought mimosas."

"And cakes!" Esther crowed, elbowing her way through. She took one look at my face. "Oh, dear."

The tears broke, and chaos ensued as only chaos can when your nearest and dearest swoop in to hold you close when your world is breaking apart ... again.

"I know a guy," Esther promised me. "We'll take care of it."

At that, I laughed. "No murdering."

"Maiming?" Meredith asked hopefully.

"No bodily harm."

Still, the thought brought a smile to my face, and despite it all, I realized that, just like before, life would go on. The last time we'd parted there had been animosity and anger involved. *We'd been young, headstrong.* Today's decision had been ... kind.

I'd survived Noah Byrne walking away from me once before, and I would do so again.

Twelve

SKYE

New Year's Eve started with towels and ended with a kidnapping.

Christmas had passed, quiet and gentle, with an empty inn and a relaxed dinner by the seaside at Rosie and Alexander's place. They had two pet puffins, Neeps and Tattie, that more than cheered up the gloom that had clung to my shoulders since Noah left.

It was almost impossible not to smile when the two small birds made a noise that sounded like a drunk man laughing softly to himself. We'd had an easy Christmas with just Harper and Reed joining us, before they went to open the pub for anyone who needed a break from family or a place to celebrate with others. I wondered what Noah was doing for Christmas.

Bloody hell, but I missed him.

More than I wanted to admit.

Even though this time was different.

Because Noah was texting me, nonstop. At first, I tried to ignore it, but he just kept texting. For a man who had an aversion to his phone, he'd suddenly seemed to discover it as his favorite way to communicate. He'd send pictures, silly jokes, or lyrics half-finished, asking for my opinion.

Sometimes I responded. Sometimes I left him on read. My heart didn't know what to think about it, so I kept my walls up, though he was slowly building a door.

By mid-morning on New Year's Eve, I had the laundry turned over, the scones made for tea, and a quiet house that felt a size too big. I had two rooms booked with short stays, and though I'd normally be full over the holidays, I was grateful for any bookings I could get. I moved through rooms checking small things because that's what I did when my brain didn't want to sit still. Extra tea bags in the blue room. Matches on the mantel. Fresh shortbread on the tray by the kettle. Every task took the edge off for five minutes and then the edge returned.

By late afternoon, I was ready to settle in with a good book, when the front bell rang like someone meant it. I opened the door to find Esther, Meredith, and Shannon on the step, lined up like a firing squad in winter coats and smug smiles. Cherise stood behind them holding a garment bag and a plastic tub of makeup.

"Happy Hogmanay," Esther announced. "We've brought your sparkle. You're coming out."

"No, I most certainly am not," I said. "I have guests."

"You have one German couple who are up at Kings-barns for a fancy meal and a woman named Eileen who has already told me she intends to be asleep by half past nine," Esther said. "We checked on our way over."

"You checked my guest list?"

"We checked with Eileen," Meredith said. "She's my second cousin. She snores like a tractor and won't hear a cannon."

"Skye," Shannon added gently, "you need a night where you wear something silly and eat food you didn't make."

"I'm not in the mood," I said. Understatement. My mood had sat down on the floor and refused to put on shoes.

"That's why we're here," Esther said, already stepping across the threshold. "Fetch your lipstick and your spine."

They didn't ask permission to come in. They took off their coats and moved like a team. Cherise unzipped the garment bag and revealed a dress. It was a deep emerald green with sparkles splashed across it and fringe at the hem. I hated how much I liked it. Where had they even found a dress like that in Kingsbarns?

"What's the theme?" I asked, because the Book Bitches never did anything without a theme.

"No theme," Meredith said at the same time Esther said, "Karaoke."

I leveled a look at Esther. "Haven't you DJed enough this month?"

"I give the people what they want." Esther sniffed.

"Where is it?" I asked. I hadn't heard about the community center being booked out.

"A house outside town," Esther said.

"Whose house?"

"Come and see," she said, which was not an answer.

"I'm not playing dress up to sit in a stranger's lounge." I put my hands on my hips.

"You need to come. Otherwise we'll just terrorize you here," Esther ordered, but then she softened a tad. "If you hate it, we'll bring you home."

I looked at all their faces. They had used this same formation on me when the pub needed painting and when they bullied the paparazzi into buying Christmas concert tickets. It worked then. It worked now.

"Fine," I said. "But I'm not wearing heels."

"Who wears heels anymore?" Cherise asked. "We've earned our comfort, dear."

They got me into the dress. Cherise did a quick updo that didn't make me look like I'd tried too hard. Shannon swiped on a lipstick that made me look like I had a pulse. Esther watched the clock and texted furiously.

"Who are you texting?" I finally asked.

"Daniel. If he's not dressed and ready, he's going to be in trouble," Esther said with a sniff.

Piling into two cars, I ended up in the passenger seat of Esther's small car while Meredith and Shannon argued quietly about whether Mr. Darcy would have worn a kilt to a Scottish ball. We left the village and took the road skirting the fields that wound along the sea. It was one of those clear nights where the air bit your nose and the stars looked like ice chips against the inky night sky.

I had lived in Kingsbarns my whole life, and I knew most of the houses, but we turned down a gravel lane I didn't recognize and rolled up to a set of stone pillars and a gate that looked like it had opinions. Beyond the gate, a drive curved through trees and delivered us to a long white house with a slate roof and a view that fell away toward the sea. It was elegant without being posh. Large windows spilled light out onto the front drive and twinkle lights threaded the bushes. Smoke curled from the chimney and disappeared into the wind.

"This is new," I said. "Or is it? I've never been down this way before."

"It was renovated a few years back. I think it's been used as an Airbnb for a while," Esther said. "It went through a few hands. It's been empty more than it's been loved."

We got out and the cold slapped me in the face, sending a shiver down my back. Something shifted inside me as I looked up at the house, an awareness, and then the door swung open.

"Skye! Don't you look lovely?" Daniel asked, looking adorable in a waistcoat and bow tie. "Here, let me take your coat."

Esther leaned in and gave Daniel a smooch before sashaying into the house like she owned it. The others followed, and I was surprised to see several people from around town already chatting away with drinks in their hands.

The room was beautiful with tall windows that faced the sea, a fire roaring in the fireplace, and done up in earthy tones that I imagined would look lovely with the ocean as a backdrop during the day.

"Did you rent this house for the party?" I asked Daniel.

"No," Daniel said. "Oh, Skye, be a dear. Can you grab Esther a Coke from the cooler? It's through there."

I turned to a door where Daniel, his hands full of coats, nodded at.

"Aye, no problem. Anything for anyone else?" I asked.

"Maybe another Coke for Cherise, as she drove."

"On it," I said, happy to have a task, as voices and music swelled around me. I wasn't ready to make idle chitchat, I'd need a drink first for that. *I really didn't want to be here.* I wanted to be at home, nursing a gin and tonic, and doing my best not to think about what Noah was doing. Turning the knob, I pushed the door open and the cold hit me once again.

"Oh, this must be a garage—"

I pulled up short to see Noah sitting in a chair, guitar on his lap, a cheap bottle of the only red wine we could afford back in the day on the table. Another chair sat empty next to him.

My heart slammed against my chest.

It was exactly the setup, albeit in a far fancier house, that we'd sat in all those years ago when we used to write songs shivering in the cold garage, our hearts open and our future before us.

He looked incredible.

I wanted to go crawl into his lap and never let go.

Instead, I let the door fall closed behind me with a definitive click, uncertain of what to do.

Noah quirked that half smile I loved so much and then my stomach twisted as he strummed the opening chords to *Skye*, his most famous and my most-hated song. I wanted to leave. To just turn around and stomp out of the house and forget that Noah Byrne ever existed.

But when he began to sing …

He'd changed the lyrics.

"Skye, believe in us, I'm betting with all my heart tonight,

Skye, sing with me and I'll be there to keep it right.
We'll build our tomorrow, chord by chord, till it shines—
Skye, say the word and I am yours for all of time."

My mouth dropped open and then I was moving across the room, staying his hand on the guitar so the chord broke off, discordant and awkward. Noah's eyes held mine.

"Do you mean it?" I asked, my throat tight.

"Every word. I love you, Skye. A part of me always has. But seeing you again? Making music together? It made me realize what was important in life. I was a fool then, but I don't have to be a fool now. I'd like to think I've learned a few lessons on the road." Noah's lips quirked up again and my heart softened.

"Is this ... is this your house?" I asked, my breath catching as he put the guitar down and stood, cupping my chin with his hand. Tilting my head up, he kissed me, long and deep, until I no longer noticed the cold of the garage and all I could think about was him. Then he broke the kiss and bent his forehead to mine, our breaths matching the same beat.

"Aye."

"You bought a house," I said. It came out halfway between accusation and admiration.

"Rented for a year with an option to buy," he said. "It came up the week I left. Matt found the listing. I asked him to put a hold on it. I didn't know if I'd have the nerve to ask you to come here otherwise."

I had about a hundred questions. Instead, I didn't ask any of them. "It's beautiful."

"Come see the bit that made me sign," he said, and then he checked himself. "If you want."

I wanted.

Opening a side door in the garage, he tugged me outside and through a stone courtyard, to a small brick outbuilding. Flinging the door open, he hit the lights and I peered into a bright space with solid walls, thick rugs on the wood floors, and two wide windows that faced the sea. The room was bare except for a couple of armchairs, and a long table covered in equipment still in boxes. Cables. Mics. A small mixing board. Acoustic panels propped against the wall.

"You're building a studio," I said, my pulse picking up speed.

"I am," he said. "A home one. Proper, but not flashy. Enough so we can record vocals and guitars and get good demos."

"We?" I asked before I could stuff the word back in my mouth.

He took a breath. "I negotiated a contract," he said. "No tour required unless I decide I want one, and even then it would be short and slow. No press junkets. We do a few pieces with people we trust. The label gets songs. They don't get my life. I made that clear. The important bit, Skye ..." He put his hand on the table like he needed something solid under it. "They want what *we* wrote. Our song. This new label loved it. They want more. I told them I would only do it if I could do it here. With you. On your schedule. When you want. *If* you want. You can keep running your inn. Always. This is not a trap. It's a room with a door you can walk out of whenever you like. But if you walk in, there's work here with your name on it. There's also a man desperately in love with you, ready to put our future first."

I listened. The words were simple but the meaning was

significant. I picked up one of the still-wrapped micro-phones and turned it in my hands to have something to look at.

"You said no," he added quietly. "I heard you. I left anyway because I needed to see if I could get the shape of this right. I came back because I think that I did."

"Do they know you're stubborn?" I asked.

"They offered me a press calendar that looked like a military exercise. I offered them a list that looked like a shopping trip," he said. "We met in the middle."

"What does 'work with your name on it' mean?"

"Writing credits. Production credit if you sit at the board and help me shape it, which you should, because you're good at telling me when I'm being a show-off. A share of the publishing on anything your words touch. If we decide to put your voice on the record, you get what a featured artist gets. If we don't, you still get paid for the writing."

"Paid," I repeated, because my brain sometimes needed a second lap.

"It's proper money," he said. "Not 'here's a voucher for crisps.' Not 'exposure.' It doesn't solve everything. But it helps when January at the inn is slow, and the boiler decides to break on the coldest day of the year."

I set the mic down then put my hands on the back of a chair because my knees felt a little loose. "I told you no."

"You did," he said. His face didn't change. He didn't flinch either.

"And you came back with a different question."
"Yes."

I looked at the windows. I couldn't see the sea, but I

could feel it in my bones. I took a few deep breaths, my thoughts whirling furiously. He waited. Somewhere along the way he had learned some patience. His expression was tight, his eyes wary as he watched me.

"I didn't want to get pulled back into your life," I said, trying to keep my voice steady. "I didn't want to vanish into it."

"Then don't," he said. "I'm asking you to let me into yours. Sometimes at a microphone. Sometimes in your kitchen with a cup of tea."

"It still scares me," I admitted.

"That's fine," he said. "We can be scared and still try."

We stood there in a room full of boxes while a party formed in the house. I could hear Shannon corralling someone into wearing a hat and Esther cajoling Daniel to give her the microphone. The sound of the party made the decision easier, not harder.

"I can't promise every week," I said. "I can't promise a marathon."

"Understood. But, my wildfire, I also didn't ask for one," he said. "I asked you to walk in sometimes and help me make something honest."

My wildfire. How I've missed him calling me that.

I nodded. My throat felt tight. "We can try."

He let out a breath like he'd been holding it since the day he left. "Okay," he said, and his voice went soft in the middle. "Okay."

And then his lips were on mine, and we were sinking, sliding, into each other, chasing the chorus line on a song we'd yet to write.

But now, at least, I knew we had time to write it. Together.

We went back to the big room because if we stayed in the quiet any longer, I might jump him on the rug. That was for later. If I knew anything about the Book Bitches, I knew we had limited time before one of them interrupted us to get the gossip. Laughing, I dragged Noah across the courtyard and back inside where the party had built itself in our absence. Coats piled on a bench. A long table strained under a mountain of food that looked like everyone in the village had emptied their fridges. Paper crowns were being passed about. Rosie had built a "Resolution Tree" out of branches in a vase and people were hanging tags on it with lies and hopes. Harper had set up a photo corner with a banner that read ... *New Year, Same Chaos.*

For the first time in days, the ache in my chest eased. I didn't know what the year would bring. I knew two things that mattered ... I could keep my life. And I could let it grow.

"Happy New Year, Skye," Noah said.

"Happy New Year," I said back, and when I tilted my head up to accept his kiss, the party went wild.

"All right, folks, you saw it here first," Esther crowed into the microphone. The opening strains of Marvin Gaye's *Let's Get It On* cued up, and I groaned into Noah's kiss, and then we broke apart, both laughing.

"Never change, Esther," I called, holding up a glass of champagne someone handed me. "Never change."

Epilogue

SKYE

"Ow!" Noah cried, as Wallace launched himself from the bar onto Noah's lap, digging his claws in. "Is this why he's called a warrior kitten?"

"No," Cherise called, looking up from where she read a book with a half-naked woman being carried by an almost entirely naked man on the cover. "It's because the warriors used to carry them into battle in their sporrans."

Noah's mouth dropped open and I bit back a grin as I cleaned some dirty glasses behind the bar.

"Aye, right they did. And me mum won gold in the Olympics." Noah glared at Cherise, certain she was having him on. Cherise just shrugged, turned a page, and went back to her smutty story. Noah turned to me, an eyebrow raised.

"Did they really?" he mouthed to me.

I burst out laughing and leaned over to scratch Wallace's wee head.

"Aye, they certainly did. Every good warrior kept a kitten with him, didn't they?"

"Surely that's not true," Noah protested.

We were both cat-sitting and pub-sitting for Harper and Reed, as they'd taken a much-needed vacation. It was February, dismal as all hell outside, and I was happy as could be.

Noah, true to his word, hadn't pressed me on the songwriting and slowly I'd been integrating myself into his world a bit more. Some nights, if I didn't have guests, I stayed over at his house. Other nights, he stayed in my wee upstairs flat with me. We'd fallen into an easy rhythm, and though sometimes my guests almost fainted when they realized that *the* Noah Byrne was having tea with them in their guesthouse, for the most part, Noah was able to live a fairly unbothered life.

He'd gotten his studio set up the way he liked, much faster than I would have expected, but I guess that's what happens when you have a butt load of money and a record contract on the line. I couldn't help but be drawn into the act of making music again. It was in my bones, after all, and I often found myself humming melodies that would pop into my head throughout the day. And Noah would be right there, sliding his voice in under mine, and every time, my heart felt full to bursting.

We weren't rushing anything. There was no real talk of what came next, or where we were going. Instead, we leaned into discovering who we were together in this moment.

And, aside from Esther deciding she needed to document it every step of the way, we were happy about it.

A flash blinded me and I sighed, turning to Esther.

"Haven't we talked about the whole not using a flash indoors, Esther?"

"But it's what all the kids are doing these days. They like these washed-out, nineties vibe, authentic photos. Like you aren't trying too hard, you know?" Esther looked up from her phone as I glared at her. She wore a jumper that said *Book Bitches for Life.*

"What kids? And I thought we talked to you about privacy." I gave her a look.

"All the kids. And I'm not taking photos of you, Miss Full of Herself. It's for wee Wallace's Instagram. He's quite famous, you know." Esther leaned down and scratched under Wallace's chin and I rolled my eyes over her head at Noah. He grinned and my stomach did that funny fluttery thing it did whenever I saw him.

"Well, you can take a picture of him with cake," I said, bringing out a cake box. Wallace, sensing food, hopped from Noah's lap to the bar and nudged his head against the box.

"What's the occasion?" Meredith called from where she read next to Cherise. The pub was half full, with quiet music playing, and a fire warming the room while icy sleet rained down outside.

"It's my gran's birthday." Reaching into my tote, I pulled out my favorite picture of her, one where she was laughing by the sea as the sun set, and put it next to the framed photo of Lewis on the counter. He already had a shot poured for him in front of his picture frame, but my gran preferred a spot of sherry, so I poured her that instead and tucked it in front of the frame.

Brrrrp. Wallace let out a soft little meow, drawing my attention, but just before I shifted, I saw her.

Gran sitting right next to Lewis, both of their faces wreathed in smiles, and then they were gone.

My heart warmed, and then twisted, in that funny way it does when someone's memory brings you both joy and a wee touch of sadness.

"Now, none of that, lass. You know I have no tolerance for all that weeping and wailing you young folk get on with." I heard her voice, clear as day, and despite myself, I snorted.

She'd always been one to put on a cup of tea and move past the emotional bits.

So I'd honor today in much the same way.

Flipping the lid over, I pulled out a knife.

"Who wants cake?" I asked.

"Me!" most of the pub cried.

And then Wallace did the unthinkable and dove his nose straight into the frosting. Noah choked on a laugh. I gasped as Wallace pulled his head back, almost startled to find frosting on his nose, and then began to lick at it hysterically.

Flashes blinded me.

"Damn it, Esther!" I said, holding my hand in front of my face.

"Oh wheesht, Skye. Do it for the 'gram."

"You're impossible." I sighed, laughing as Wallace tried to lick all the frosting from his face. When a gleam entered the cat's eye, I angled the box away.

"Right, who wants slightly smushed cake with a side of a few cat hairs?"

Laughter greeted me and I smiled back, happy that for once, my fresh start had led me where I needed to go all along.

Back to Noah.

His eyes met mine over the cake box, easy and rested, a world of difference from the soul-weary ones when he'd first slipped through my door before Christmas.

He was home now.

We were home now. Together.

We were finally writing our story, the song that had never been written, and it was, if I do say so myself, perfect.

Looking for added sparkle and fun this Christmas? Be sure to order one of these limited edition Christmas Coo designs! I will be wearing the All I want for Christmas is Moo design when I visit family in Scotland this December. Keep an eye out for pictures in my newsletter and on social media. Sparkle on!

Shop today at triciaomalley.myshopify.com

Christmas Coo
Collection
www.triciaomalley.com

All I want for Christmas is moo
CHILLIN'
WITH MY
SNOWMIES
SANTA COOS
IS COMING
TO TOWN

Sneak Peek

Delicious banter, bookstore magic, adorable puffins, and a heartwarmingly happily-ever-after makes this an enchanting Christmas treat.

Read on for a sneak peek!

Highland Hearts Holiday Bookshop

ROSIE

"Y̲ou're going to have a riot on your hands."

I eyed the line outside, where a group of deter-mined women crowded by the door, a few going so far as to bang on the store windows. My shoulders tensed. These women were out for blood. This was a "take no prisoners" situation. I could see it in their eyes. The thrill of the hunt ran through them, and they would eat me for breakfast.

This was my worst nightmare.

I hadn't signed up for this.

I mean, I worked here, so *technically* I had. If you can call my employment via emotional manipulation from my boyfriend's family a choice. I only worked at Davidson's Discount Store because I was dating the owner's son and somehow hadn't put up a fight when they had insisted I join the family retail business after losing my job as a tech writer for a medical systems company. It was a toss-up which job had bored me more, but at least the tech writing gig had been virtual, and I had *actually* used my degree. Alas, the higher-ups had frowned on my comparing the sound of snoring to a dragon's roar to describe the benefits of a sleep apnea device. Apparently, I had a history of sprinkling in references to magickal elements far more than I'd been aware of, and I'd been quietly asked to leave with the suggestion that I stick to creative writing.

When John's family had immediately insisted I join them at Davidson's Discount—*because that's what family does, Rose*—I hadn't had the energy to say no. Frankly, I hadn't had the energy to do much, of late, and it had just been easier to go along with it when they gave me an apron and a key to the shop.

That being said, taking the easy way out was starting to look a lot like I was about to get mauled for the latest trending color of a forty-ounce water bottle. Apparently, TikTok had kicked off the need for a mustard-colored water bottle with neon pink writing on it, and for some unknown reason we were the only store in the metro area to get a shipment of them.

What had my life become?

When had I stopped caring enough to voice my opinion? To stand up for myself? Lately I felt it was just easier to say nothing because everyone else's voices had grown so much louder.

And what I really craved was the quiet.

A lovely quiet life.

Without fluorescent lighting and neon discount price stickers.

Without my bland boyfriend who I held on to because I was afraid of change. Of rocking the boat. Of doing ... anything, really. Nothing had lit me up, excited me, got my juices running, so to speak, in ages. I could feel, down to the very marrow of my bones, that I needed to make a change. But I just hadn't been able to bring myself to do it. Not yet. Maybe if I had some direction or found a passion that excited me, then I'd finally work up the courage to walk away from Davidson's Discount Store and the tedium of selling products I cared little for. *They didn't even have a book section*.

Everyone said you needed to take the bull by the horns, but have you seen bulls? They're terrifying. I was so *not* the type to wave a red flag at my future. Couldn't courage come in the form of a thousand tiny steps neatly written out on a checklist in my color-coded and indexed notebook?

I eyed the feral women outside.

Where did they get their energy? Maybe I could bottle some of it and it would make me become bold and fearsome, ready to take on the world and *Do Exciting Things* with my life. Yes, I saw that in all caps, like when I scrolled Instagram and saw everyone out *Living Their Big Lives*. Maybe I didn't need a big life, but I definitely needed a different one.

A buzzer sounded and I choked, taking a step back.

"Now, Rose, you'll want to stand here to greet everyone."

Still, he called me Rose. No matter how many times I'd asked him to call me Rosie. Even my mother had deemed me bland as an infant and had graced me with the deplorable name of Rose Withers. Getting people to call me Rosie had been a lifelong battle, but it was my small attempt at growth—like a flower reaching for sunshine instead of withering into sadness like my name suggested.

John's hand came up and squeezed the back of my neck, and I looked up at him in disbelief.

"*Greet*? John, there's no greeting. They're going to run us over and beat us over the head with their purses until they get every one of these cups. The smartest thing we can do is move out of the way and let them at it."

"But we need to tell them about our early Black Friday deals."

They don't care about your crappy deals on your crappy mass-produced crap, I wanted to shout at him. Instead, I pasted a fake customer service smile on my face and gripped my hands behind my back, digging my nails into my sweaty palms.

John's father unlocked the doors.

Crappity crap.

"Ladies, welcome to—"

Before he could finish the sentence, he was knocked to his knees by an overzealous woman sporting three totes and the single-minded determination that only a quad espresso from Starbucks could give you.

"Dad!" It was too late. John pushed against the crowd, but it was like trying to swim against a Tsunami. When he took a shopping basket to the crotch, I winced as he went down, a long keening noise escaping his mouth. The women behind him leapt over him, mirroring Olympic hurdlers, and thundered toward the display of water bottles.

"Right this way, ladies," I said, stepping way back and sweeping an arm out to point in the direction of the water bottle display. The idiots had placed the display at the back of the store, seeming to think that buyers would wander the shop and check out the other deals on their way to their destination. Instead, the crowd blasted past racks of Christmas decorations, Thanksgiving knickknacks, and boxes of wrapping paper. When a display of ornaments went flying, I sighed and stepped farther back and away from the pandemonium.

I couldn't find it in myself to care about the chaos that was currently unraveling the store like someone had tossed a bouncy ball into a crystal shop. I'd quietly voiced my opinions at the staff meeting, pointing out that a ticketing system, or even just a table directly at the front of the store, would be the most seamless route to sell these bottles, but my thoughts had been immediately dismissed. As usual. It had been easier to bury my nose back in a book, nodding at the right times, than to point out how stupid they were being with their planning. Now, as John hobbled across the store to help his father off the floor, I shrugged.

I should feel bad for them. And in a loose sort of human way, I did. I never liked to see people get hurt. But since they were both up and walking, it didn't seem like too much damage had been done, so I wouldn't waste more energy caring. Just the right amount to not make me a sociopath, I decided, and slipped further out of their sight, not wanting to hear what they'd order me to do next. Instead, I walked down a long aisle full of kitchenware and household goods, trying to ignore how the screams from the crowd sent the hair on the back of my neck standing.

I liked people.

I swear I liked people.

I just liked them in small doses.

Small *quiet* doses.

Preferably when talking about books, playing board games, or in online forums that required little face-to-face interaction. It wasn't that I was shy, necessarily, I'd just always found solace with a book in front of my face, and somehow along the way that had become a wall of sorts between me and the outside world. One which I dearly wished I could put up now, as I gingerly crept toward the shouts in the back of the store. Should I even try to do anything to help? What could I possibly say to break up a fight? I'd never even *seen* a fight in real life.

With the thought of seeing my first real fight piquing my curiosity, I picked up my pace, reaching for my phone to snap a few photos for my best friend, Jessica. She'd eat this up, that was for sure, and I could already hear her harassing me if I didn't get footage of this. She was always yammering on about going viral and whatnot, but the only viral things I cared about were advanced reader copies from my favorite fantasy authors.

Hitting record and lifting my phone, I turned the corner at the end of the aisle and entered chaos. One woman lifted her tote bag and smacked another across the face with it, while a third grabbed two of the water bottles out of the other's tote, and turning, she raised them in the air in victory. Without looking, she barreled away from the crowd.

In other words, directly at me.

I only had a moment to squeak out a warning cry before a mustard-yellow water bottle with *Boujee Bitch* written on it caught me in the eye.

And then everything went black.

Read Today!

Author's Note

I can't believe we are already at Christmas time again this year. For me, this has been a year of huge changes. I honestly wasn't even sure I'd have time to fit in a wee Christmas story for everyone, so I was really happy that I was able to sneak this novella in featuring some of our favorite characters. I wrote this while hunkered down in a cottage by the seaside in Denmark, and I was delighted to have some time to simply focus and write.

This year we made the big change from living in the Caribbean to going nomadic, and it has been a huge adjustment. Since we've sold our house, we've been to Belfast, London, Edinburgh, Glasgow, Denmark, Ireland, and as I write this, we're in Florence. And while I am greatly enjoying our time on the road, there is something about winter time that makes me want to cozy in and stay rooted.

I know this time of year can be tricky for many, particularly those who are grieving a loss, and I want to ask that you keep your light shining for others. You'd be surprised at the kindness that still exists in this world, and I see it on every friendly face I meet on my travels. At the end of the day, we all just want to share a smile with a friend. So to that, I would like to send you all a smile and loads of sparkles, to keep you shining through these winter months.

Sparkle on, friends!

Tricia O'Malley

Author's Acknowledgement

A very deep and heartfelt *thank you* goes to those in my life who have continued to support me on this wonderful journey of being an author. At times, this job can be very stressful, however, I'm grateful to have the sounding board of my friends who help me through the trickier moments of self-doubt. An extra-special thanks goes to The Scotsman, who is my number one supporter and always manages to make me smile.

Please know that every book I write is a part of me, and I hope you feel the love that I put into my stories. Without my readers, my work means nothing, and I am grateful that you all are willing to share your valuable time with the worlds I create. I hope each book brings a smile to your face and for just a moment it gives you a much-needed escape.

THE WILDSONG SERIES

Song of the Fae

Melody of Flame

Chorus of Ashes

Lyric of Wind

"The magic of Fae is so believable. I read these books in one sitting
and can't wait for the next one. These are books you will reread
many times."

- Amazon Review

A completed series in Kindle Unlimited.

Available in audio, e-book & paperback!

THE SIREN ISLAND SERIES

Good Girl

Up to No Good

A Good Chance

Good Moon Rising

Too Good to Be True

A Good Soul

In Good Time

A completed series in Kindle Unlimited.

Available in audio, e-book & paperback!

"Love her books and was excited for a totally new and different one! Once again, she did NOT disappoint! Magical in multiple ways and on multiple levels. Her writing style, while similar to that of Nora Roberts, kicks it up a notch!! I want to visit that island, stay in the B&B and meet the gals who run it! The characters are THAT real!!!" - Amazon Review

THE ALTHEA ROSE SERIES

One Tequila

Tequila for Two

Tequila Will Kill Ya (Novella)

Three Tequilas

Tequila Shots & Valentine Knots (Novella)

Tequila Four

A Fifth of Tequila

A Sixer of Tequila

Seven Deadly Tequilas

Eight Ways to Tequila

Tequila for Christmas (Novella)

"Not my usual genre but couldn't resist the Florida Keys setting. I was hooked from the first page. A fun read with just the right amount of crazy! Will definitely follow this series."- Amazon Review

A completed series in Kindle Unlimited.

Available in audio, e-book & paperback!

STAND ALONE NOVELS

<u>Love's a Witch</u>

She's got runaway magic. He's got a town to protect. Too bad fate has other plans.

<u>Highland Hearts Holiday Bookshop</u>

As Christmas looms, and lonely hearts beg for love, I'm tossed into the world of magic and romance, aided by a meddling book club who seems more interested in romance than reading.

<u>Ms. Bitch</u>

"Ms. Bitch is sunshine in a book! An uplifting story of fighting your way through heartbreak and making your own version of happily-ever-after."

~Ann Charles, USA Today Bestselling Author

<u>Starting Over Scottish</u>

Grumpy. Meet Sunshine.

She's American. He's Scottish. She's looking for a fresh start. He's returning to rediscover his roots.

<u>One Way Ticket</u>

A funny and captivating beach read where booking a one-way ticket to paradise means starting over, letting go, and taking a chance on love...one more time

10 out of 10 - The BookLife Prize

Contact Me

I hope my books have added a little magick into your life. If you have a moment to add some to my day, you can help by telling your friends and leaving a review. Word-of-mouth is the most powerful way to share my stories. Thank you.

Love books? What about fun giveaways? Nope? Okay, can I entice you with underwater photos and cute dogs? Let's stay friends! Sign up for my newsletter and contact me at my website.

www.triciaomalley.com

Or find me on Facebook and Instagram.
@triciaomalleyauthor